AVAILABLE NOW!

LEARNING TO RIDE

City girl Madeline Harper never wanted to love a cowboy. But rodeo king Tanner Callen might change her mind...and win her heart.

THE McCULLAGH INN IN MAINE

Chelsea O'Kane escapes to Maine to build a new life—until she runs into Jeremy Holland, an old flame....

BOOK**SHOTS**

CROSS KILL

Along Came a Spider killer Gary Soneji died years ago. But Alex Cross swears he sees Soneji gun down his partner. Is his greatest enemy back from the grave?

ZOO II

Humans are evolving into a savage, new species that could save civilization—or end it. James Patterson's *Zoo* was just the beginning.

THE TRIAL

An accused killer will do anything to disrupt his own trial, including a courtroom shocker that Lindsay Boxer and the Women's Murder Club will never see coming.

LITTLE BLACK DRESS

Can a little black dress change everything? What begins as one woman's fantasy is about to go too far.

UPCOMING BOOKSHOTS FLAMES ROMANCES

SACKING THE QUARTERBACK

Attorney Melissa St. James wins every case. Now, when she's defending football superstar Grayson Knight, her heart is on the line, too.

DAZZLING: THE DIAMOND TRILOGY, PART I

To support her artistic career, Siobhan Dempsey works at the elite Stone Room in New York City...never expecting to be swept away by Derick Miller.

RADIANT: THE DIAMOND TRILOGY, PART II

After an explosive breakup with her billionaire boyfriend, Siobhan moves to Detroit to pursue her art. But Derick isn't ready to give her up.

BODYGUARD

Special Agent Abbie Whitmore has only one task: protect Congressman Jonathan Lassiter from a violent cartel's threats. Yet she's never had to do it while falling in love....

UPCOMING BOOKSHOTS THRILLERS.

LET'S PLAY MAKE-BELIEVE

Christy and Marty just met, and it's love at first sight. Or is it? One of them is playing a dangerous game—and only one will survive.

CHASE

A man falls to his death in an apparent accident....But why does he have the fingerprints of another man who is already dead? Detective Michael Bennett is on the case.

HUNTED

Someone is luring men from the streets to play a mysterious high-stakes game. Former Special Forces officer David Shelley goes undercover to shut it down—but will he win?

113 MINUTES

Molly Rourke's son has been murdered. Now she'll do whatever it takes to get justice. No one should underestimate a mother's love....

$10,000,000 MARRIAGE PROPOSAL

A mysterious billboard offering $10 million to get married intrigues three single women in LA. But who is Mr. Right…and is he the perfect match for the lucky winner?

THE FRENCH KISS

It's hard enough to move to a new city, but now everyone French detective Luc Moncrief cares about is being killed off. Welcome to New York.

KILLER CHEF

Caleb Rooney knows how to do two things: run a food truck and solve a murder. When people suddenly start dying of foodborne illnesses, the stakes are higher than ever….

THE CHRISTMAS MYSTERY

Two stolen paintings disappear from a Park Avenue murder scene—French detective Luc Moncrief is in for a merry Christmas.

BLACK & BLUE

Detective Harry Blue is determined to take down the serial killer who's abducted several women, but her mission leads to a shocking revelation.

SHE NEVER EXPECTED TO FALL IN LOVE WITH A COWBOY....

Rodeo king Tanner Callen isn't looking to be tied down anytime soon. When he sees Madeline Harper at a local honky-tonk—even though everything about her screams New York City—he brings out every trick in his playbook to take her home.

But soon he learns that he doesn't just want her for a night.

Instead, he hopes for forever.

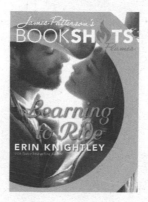

Read the heartwarming new romance
Learning to Ride, **available from**

BookShots / Little, Brown and Company
Hachette Book Group
1290 Avenue of the Americas, New York, NY 10104
bookshots.com

First Edition: July 2016

BookShots is an imprint of Little, Brown and Company, a division of Hachette Book Group, Inc. The Little, Brown name and logo are trademarks of Hachette Book Group, Inc. The BookShots name and logo are trademarks of JBP Business, LLC.

The publisher is not responsible for websites (or their content) that are not owned by the publisher.

The Hachette Speakers Bureau provides a wide range of authors for speaking events. To find out more, go to hachettespeakersbureau.com or call (866) 376-6591.

ISBN 978-0-316-32011-5
LCCN 2016935246

10 9 8 7 6 5 4 3 2 1

RRD-C

Printed in the United States of America

FOREWORD

When I first had the idea for BookShots, I knew that I wanted to include romantic stories. The whole point of BookShots is to give people lightning-fast reads that completely capture them for just a couple of hours—so publishing romance felt right.

I have a lot of respect for romance authors. I took a stab at the genre when I wrote *Suzanne's Diary for Nicholas* and *Sundays at Tiffany's*. While I was happy with the results, I learned that the process of writing those stories required hard work and dedication.

That's why I wanted to pair up with the best romance authors for BookShots. I work with writers who know how to draw emotions out of their characters, all while catapulting their plots forward.

It's been fun working on *The McCullagh Inn in Maine* with Jen McLaughlin. She wanted to weave a suspense plot through this otherwise peaceful story of redemption, and I think she did a top-notch job of blending both of those worlds in one cohesive piece. Our heroine, Chelsea

O'Kane, is stubborn, strong, and a little rough around the edges, but when she becomes reacquainted with her soul mate, Jeremy, you'll get to see her heart soften—and it's a pretty spectacular view.

James Patterson

The McCullagh Inn in Maine

Chapter 1

THE SICKLY SWEET scent of dying roses drifted over me as I backed down the driveway, moving too quickly to check for traffic first. My heart raced faster than the engine of the stolen Volvo XC90 as I stepped on the gas. All good plans allow for improvisation, right?

My fingernails were digging into the wheel. I forced myself to relax. There was no room for weakness, for panic, in my life. Not anymore. Whatever lay ahead was guaranteed to be better than what I was leaving behind, and it certainly couldn't be worse than what I'd already survived.

I took a deep breath and held it as I ran a red light, feeling more alive, more like myself, than I had in years. A horn blasted, and I gripped the wheel hard. It was a miracle I didn't break my swollen knuckles off at the joints. I was temporarily blinded by the oncoming headlights and I instinctively stepped on the gas, tensing as a truck headed directly for my door. The lights veered left and the pickup skidded off the road and into someone's yard. Not my fault, not my problem.

I never wanted it to turn out this way. Sure, I saw the writing on the wall, kept a bag packed, and made contingency plans, but I was supposed to just disappear. Vanish into the night, be an unsolved mystery. Instead, I was going to have to spend the next couple of days fleeing for my life, hoping no one put two and two together. If I could just make it to the inn…

I screeched onto the ramp for I-95 with the scent of burning rubber filling the car, but I didn't slow, not hesitating as I headed toward safety. *North*. I wouldn't stop until I reached the one place where I knew I could escape. The same place I fled from years ago, with dreams of being something—some*one*—else. I was older now, and wiser, and I'd learned people never change. My current circumstances proved that point. All you could do was play the cards you were dealt.

No one would think to look for me in the sleepy Maine town I'd once called home, the one I'd erased from my record.

I'd sworn never to go back.

Sirens wailed at a distance, and I eased up on the gas pedal, forcing myself to obey speed limits. The last thing I needed was to get pulled over right now.

Once I put a little more distance between me and Miami, I'd find a rest stop, change my clothes, and wash up.

Dyeing my brown hair could wait until I found some hole-in-the-wall to stop at for the night. I'd go blond. No one would expect me to go for that color. I hated blondes.

They led charmed lives the rest of us could only dream about.

My phone lit up, the screen showing a picture from my former life. I cursed. Keeping my eyes on the road, on that horizon, I fumbled around on the seat until I found the phone. Grabbing it, I chucked it out the window. A glance in the rearview mirror showed it disappearing under the wheels of a semi.

I gave a quick look at the object still remaining on the seat. My fingers flexed on the steering wheel. If I could only get rid of the gun the same way....

This hadn't been the plan, but then again, neither was murder.

Chapter 2

IT'D TAKEN TWO days of back-roads driving before I reached North Carolina. Ditching the car, I hopped on a bus for twelve hours. I looked like a preppy sorority sister going home for the weekend, my society persona left behind with the car. Once I hit the Maine border, I hitchhiked to the nearest used car dealer and bought a rusted old Chevy with some of the cash I'd stolen.

My destination was Hudson, Maine, which was only listed on the most thorough maps, a tiny pinprick of ink among shades of green. If you've ever heard people tell jokes about towns where the wild animals outnumber the humans, it's possible they were talking about Hudson.

This late in the season, most of the autumn leaves had dropped, and the nearly bald tires of my junker car crunched over pine cones as I navigated roads I hadn't seen in years. Finally, I arrived at the only home I'd ever known, the McCullagh Inn. My aunt, who'd owned it, had died six months ago, leaving me the business. I hadn't been able to go to the funeral, but I knew a heaven-sent opportunity when it arrived, and so I'd made discreet arrangements to keep the lights on and get a cleaning service to come through once a week.

I'd never told anyone down in Miami about the inn or my life before I arrived there, so if I had any luck left in my bones, no one would search for me here. Sure, it might seem like someone could track me down easily enough, but I came from a long line of less-than-law-abiding folks. There were ways to muddy the water.

My father had taught me to prepare for all outcomes. I knew how to fade off the face of the planet so no one ever found you again. I'd done it once before, when I ran away from home. But now I was back....

And I couldn't shake the feeling that this was where I was supposed to be all along.

I flipped the TV on, muting it as I dialed my brother on the burner phone I'd bought at a Virginia convenience store. I may have tried to go straight, but Paul had stayed in the family business.

I turned away from the morning news and caught a glimpse of myself in the tarnished, ornate mirror over the fireplace. The pale green walls of the foyer and the wood paneling of the living room weren't doing a damn thing for my complexion, and I could see the faintest shadow of a bruise beneath the makeup I'd slathered on. As I listened to the phone ring, I looked into my own blue eyes, wondering if I knew the person looking back at me. Then I turned back to the news, watching to see if what had happened in Miami had gone national. My newly blond hair swung in its ponytail. I really should've cut it, but, hey, even a girl like me is entitled to some vanities.

"Hello?" My brother's raspy voice cut through the cheap phone.

I closed my eyes for a second, nostalgia making my throat ache. Or it could've been the abuse my vocal cords had recently taken. Nothing had a greater hold on you than family. "Paul?"

"Yeah?" Silence. A lot of silence. And then: "Chelsea? Is that you?"

I licked my lips. "Yes."

"You're alive," he said flatly.

"Yes," I said again, staring at the old tree outside the front window, next to the driveway.

"I'm going to kill—"

"Paul." I swallowed again, eyeing the whiskey I'd brought out from the kitchen. It would hurt in the morning, but it might be worth the pain. "I need help, and I need you not to tell anyone I called, or where I am."

There was no hesitation. "What do you need?"

Relief hit me in the chest. It was true what they said about family. "A new ID. A completely new identity, actually."

"You're on the run. Again." At my silence, he sucked in

a breath. I'd learned at a young age that people would say anything to fill a silence. "Did you dye your hair yet?"

"Yeah."

"Nice." He sighed. "What happened, Chels?"

A phantom gunshot filled the empty inn, and for a second, I was back in that moment. I eyed the table by the front door, where I'd shoved the gun in case I needed it again. It would've been smarter to ditch it, but it was the best protection I had right now.

When the silence continued to stretch, Paul cleared his throat. "Where are you?"

I thought of the bruises I was trying to hide, the secrets I carried, and I knew my older brother would see right through me. I had no choice. I needed that ID. It was the only way I'd get my fresh start. "I'm at Aunt May McCullagh's inn, *my* inn."

There was a brief pause.

"The lawyers found you," he said.

Ignoring the accusation in his tone, I focused on the cloudy skies above the Atlantic Ocean. I'd left all the shades drawn except for one on the bay window overlooking the cliff, where a trail led down to the beach. On either side of the trail was an overgrown garden, filled with lobelia. I'd spent half my life sitting in that window, reading and looking at the storms raging over the ocean while dreaming of a future away from this tiny town. "Yeah, I know. I suck."

"No argument here," he grumbled. I could picture him sitting behind the wheel of his car, glowering at nothing in particular. Paul was happiest unhappy. "She left the inn to you, wanting you to fix it up and breathe new life into the place. She never gave up hope that someday, you'd come walking through those doors alive."

I remained silent again, because, really, what was there to say? The past was done. I couldn't go back and fix it, even if I wanted to. And those mistakes, those choices I'd made, had turned me into the woman I was. I couldn't regret that. Now I was here, ready and willing to make a new life for myself. And I'd make this the best damn inn in all of Maine.

Like a phoenix, I'd be reborn once Chelsea O'Kane was dead.

He sighed, dragging the sound out longer than a wave crashing on the shore. "Look. I'll get you what you're asking for. Meet me at Joe's to discuss it." There was a beat of silence. "It's the coffee shop on Main Street, in case you forgot."

How could I forget?

Main Street was the only street in town with any shops. There was a coffee shop, a church, a liquor store, a grocery store, a bar, and a Rite Aid. They were all on one block, with enchanting brick facades and quaint dark-gray clapboard on the old buildings. "When?"

"An hour from now. Don't be late."

Exactly an hour later, I walked down Main Street. The second I saw its Victorian architecture, I was comforted by its familiarity. But I tugged my baseball hat down to shadow my face and looked at the cracked sidewalks to avoid the usual small-town curiosity that would inevitably be thrown my way. I was always good at blending in, and I congratulated myself for not losing my touch...until I bounced off a brick wall.

Or, rather, a man.

His muscular arms closed around me, saving me from hitting the ground. The second his skin touched mine, a bolt of desire mixed with the panic that shot through my veins. I jerked back sharply, stumbling backward, and glanced up. The tall man who caught me was handsome, his wavy brown hair swept back off his face, and it was like the ground opened beneath me when I recognized him. Suddenly, that bolt of longing made perfect sense.

Oh, for God's sake. I couldn't catch a break. I'd had more than enough drama to fill ten seasons of a soap opera, and all I wanted was to lie low and nurse my injuries, but *nooo*.

It was Jeremy fricking Holland.

Damn it, he wasn't supposed to *be* here.

Chapter 3

JEREMY HOLLAND HAD been an object of infatuation since childhood—from the time I understood the difference between boys and girls up until college. He'd been a major part of my "wish on a star" phase. We'd been best friends, the kind who were supposed to be secretly in love with each other, so when he got together with the preppy blond cheerleader Mary Walker, I was pissed. When he went and proposed to her like the idiot he was, I skipped town the night before their wedding. I hadn't planned to return.

And I hadn't spoken to him since.

I may have googled him from time to time, though. Last I'd heard, he was living in Bangor, dribbling his life away at some desk job.

His gaze met mine, and the casual look in his familiar green eyes brightened to recognition. I quickly turned away—like I should have done the second I realized it was him. My heart raced, and the old undeniable attraction between us jerked back to life like a tangible thing, all because our bodies had bumped against each other on the street.

Damn his muscular arms.

And damn his outdated online profile.

"Sorry," I mumbled, sidestepping his large frame and tugging the baseball hat even lower so he wouldn't stop me. I didn't need this. Not now.

I didn't want him to focus on me.

He easily stepped the same way as me, blocking my escape effortlessly. "Are you okay?"

"Yeah." I cleared my throat, forcing my voice to drop a few octaves. Between that and my altered appearance, maybe he wouldn't recognize me. He'd married Mary, after all. How smart could he be? "I'm fine."

I walked past him, making sure not to brush against him. The last thing I needed was to feel a pull toward him. I was more panicked than I had been during my entire journey from Miami.

"Chelsea?" he asked, his voice dipping sexily. "Is that you?"

I stiffened, a few choice curse words flitting through my brain. But I bit them back, because nothing indicated guilt more than freaking out—and my father had trained me better than that. "Who?" I asked without turning around.

"Chelsea. Chelsea O'Kane."

I shook my head, balling my fists at my sides, ignoring

the way his voice made me feel. All shivery, broken, and empty. "Never heard of her, but I hope she's pretty if you've got us confused."

As I attempted to saunter away, forcing myself to unclench my fists and keep my body language relaxed, he called out, "No matter how hard your daddy tried to teach you, you always were a lousy liar, Chels. Drop the act, and turn around."

I took a deep breath and considered my options. If I kept walking, Jeremy would come after me, and the ensuing argument would draw more attention than I wanted. If I faced him, I risked getting sucked back into his "help your fellow man" world, and right now, I could only help one person—myself.

Luckily for me, I saw Paul's truck turn the corner of Main and Birch. "Whoever you thought I was, trust me, that girl is long gone."

There was an intake of breath from behind me and I paused, for the briefest of moments, at the sound. I wanted so badly to turn around, to run into his arms and tell him everything that was bothering me, like I'd done when we were kids, but then my self-preservation instincts kicked in. I crossed the street, not bothering to look both ways—in this town, I'd hear a car well before it ever reached me.

Paul's truck pulled up to the curb of the coffee shop, and I yanked the door open at the same time as he opened his, one foot out the door. He glanced at me in surprise. "I thought we were—"

"Change of plans," I growled. "Drive. Fast."

He frowned, closing his door without hesitation. "Is that—?"

"Yep," I gritted out. "And he recognized me."

"Shit," Paul said, jerking the truck into drive. "He won't let it go at one conversation."

"I know." I scanned our surroundings through the passenger window, sucking in a breath. "Son of a bitch."

Damn it, why did I have such lousy taste in men? The recognition in Jeremy's eyes scared me more than Richard's fists ever had. If I wasn't careful, Jeremy would ruin everything....

And then I'd be the one facing down the barrel of a gun.

Chapter 4

PAUL TURNED DOWN the road that led to the inn, a ramshackle gem framed by old forest. His grip on the wheel was unyielding. He stared out the windshield, flexing his jaw, ignoring me. More than likely he was about to spout the perfect reprimand for this situation—one he'd probably been rehearsing since I'd left. "You look like shit."

"Thanks," I said dryly.

"Where did the bruises come from?"

Of course he saw them. "A problem that no longer exists."

He pressed his mouth into a tight line. "What did Jeremy say?"

"He asked if I was Chelsea O'Kane. I told him I wasn't."

"That was stupid," Paul snapped. "Now he'll be focused on you and why you lied. You need to shake him off."

I dropped my head back on the seat. Damn it, he was right. And I didn't need that kind of attention right now—especially not from *him*. "I'll find him. Tell him I want nothing to do with him and ask him to leave me alone. He will."

Paul snorted. "Yeah. Sure he will."

"He will," I said, knowing it was true. Jeremy had picked Mary, after all.

There were new wrinkles around Paul's eyes, signs of a life filled with laughter and worry earned while I'd been away, which made me feel a little emptier inside. Otherwise, he had the same brown hair and blue eyes that were, as always, tinged with something between a touch of mischief and anger at the world.

"What the hell did you get yourself into this time?" he asked.

I shook my head, staring out the window at the trees blurring together as we sped by, my mind still on Jeremy and the threat he posed. I hoped he dropped the idea of reconnecting and disappeared out of my life again. "You don't need to know the details."

"The hell I don't," he growled. "You're blond, Chels. *Blond*. Obviously, shit got real."

Wincing, I touched my hair self-consciously. I looked ridiculous in this color and we both knew it. "The less you know, the better. Just trust me on this."

"But—" He sighed. "Whatever."

I swallowed and glanced in the rearview to make sure we didn't have a tail.

"You have to admit it's pretty shitty that you disappeared

from my life, only to show up when you need me to get you a new ID, so you can...what? Run again?" he snapped.

"I don't just need a new ID," I said softly. "I need Chelsea O'Kane to be legally pronounced dead. And after that, I'm not going anywhere."

He braked, the tires squealing softly at the sudden movement, and slowly turned to me. *"Dead?"*

I nodded once, knowing I was asking for a lot, but it was the only way I stood a chance at coming out of this mess alive. "Can you do that?"

He stepped on the gas, pulling into the inn's circular gravel driveway without answering, but I didn't make the mistake of assuming his silence was a good thing. I knew better than that. The second he put the truck into park, he turned to me, scowling. "I understood why you ran. You wanted to get away from this life, from Dad's legacy. You wanted to be clean. Normal. *Legit*. Right?"

That had been the plan, yeah. But apparently, I wasn't the type of girl who got clean. Gripping my knees, I nodded, still not speaking.

Paul needed to say his piece, and I intended to let him.

"So you ran, and you never called or told me where you were. I didn't even know if you were still alive."

I stared at the faded gray clapboard and peeling blue shutters on the front of the house. The gardens were choked with weeds, but renovating the inside was my first priority. "I'm sorry. I was living in Miami, working as a lawyer, when things went…" I trailed off and made the *ka-boom* motion with my hands.

"A lawyer, huh?" He stared at me, his gaze filled with pain and accusation. "You can't get any more legit than a lawyer. Can't remove yourself from this family any further than that, right, Chels? The only thing worse would've been becoming a cop."

"I'd never—" I stared down at my legs. That's exactly what I'd been thinking when I chose my major. I'd been so desperate to be a better person. That had been all Jeremy's fault. Him and his do-good attitude that never faltered. "I mean, right."

"And now you're here, asking for a favor.…" The crisp wind, carrying the taste of salt water, buffeted the overhanging branches, casting shadows on his face. Paul continued, "Asking for *my* help."

I nodded, grabbing hold of my knees.

While I'd done what needed to be done, I was older now, and I never should have cut ties with my brother, no matter what he did for a living. No matter how similar he was to our father.

Coming home to Maine meant safety, but it also meant a chance to start over, to rebuild my relationship with my brother. I needed him and this inn.

"Tell me, Chels. Was it worth it? Did you find what you were looking for?"

"No. Is that what you want to hear? I thought I could

be someone who made a difference in the world, who changed things for the better, but all I did was make things worse. So that's why I came home to the inn, to you. To start over. Again."

Paul rubbed his forehead, letting out a sardonic laugh. "How far up shit creek are you? You going to end up in jail like Dad?"

"This isn't some penny-ante con man scam." I pressed my lips together and shrugged. "If I get caught? Well, let's put it this way. You'll never find the pieces."

Stiffening, he dropped his hand. "Jesus."

"Can you do it or not?"

He tapped his fingers on his thigh. "It's not going to be easy. Declaring someone dead takes a shitload of paperwork." He let out a long breath, drawing it out. "But I have some connections in Bangor who can pull it off, as well as the name change."

I collapsed against the headrest. "Thank you."

"After you're 'dead,' what then? You got a plan?"

"I do what I should have done all along." I gestured at the inn, eyeing the mildewing posts on the wrap-around porch. "Fix this place up. Open for business. Make Aunt May proud. *Stay*."

He cocked a brow. "And when people ask why your last name is different?"

"Divorce." I twisted my lips. "Or maybe I'm widowed. Whichever draws less curiosity."

"Divorced, I think," he said hesitantly. "You're really staying?"

"Yes. I'm done running. Whatever happens, happens. This is where I make my stand."

"All right." He nodded, placed his hands on the wheel, gripping it tightly. "How do you want to die?"

Chapter 5

THAT NIGHT, I turned on the big-screen TV. Settling into the corner of the couch with my glass of whiskey, I tucked myself in with an afghan Aunt May had crocheted. My notebook of lists and plans for the inn's renovation slid between me and the couch. I smiled at the roaring fire I'd managed to get going before focusing on CNN, which was covering a bombing in Kuwait.

Not a shooting in Miami.

I hadn't eaten all day, but that was okay because I wasn't really hungry. I didn't need food, just some whiskey to help me survive the night ahead. Anything to help me sleep, without knocking me out so deeply I couldn't hear danger approaching.

Even an hour of shut-eye would be nice.

Rubbing my face, I yawned and set my drink down. I froze when someone knocked. The only person who knew I was here was Paul, and he was in Bangor taking care of my identity crisis.

Heart pounding, I stood on the scratched hardwood floors, slowly creeping forward. A floorboard squeaked under my foot and I half expected to hear gunshots, but only silence followed. I opened the drawer I'd slid my gun into, resting my fingers on the cool barrel of the Glock.

Pulling the curtains back hesitantly, I peeked outside. And damned if I didn't want to use that gun even more than before. Gritting my teeth, I let the doorknob go, glowering out the tiny slit of the curtain opening. *Fricking* Jeremy Holland. He stood underneath the flickering light on the porch, holding food and a bottle of wine, the soft amber glow making him look too hot for my liking.

There was no way in hell I was letting him in.

He rocked back on his heels and knocked again. When I didn't move, he grinned and leaned in close to the door. "I can hear you breathing."

I winced, covering my mouth, which was stupid, because unless he'd become a superhero over the years, he was lying.

"I know you're in there, Chelsea O'Kane. Open up."

Announce my identity to the whole world, why don't ya?

I hesitated, pressing my hand against the door. What were the chances of him giving up and going away? Slim to none. Jeremy would never give up on anything so long as the slightest shred of hope remained.

"I have your favorite Chinese food. General Tso's

chicken, rice, egg rolls, and red wine." He waited, and when I didn't unlock the door, he sighed. "If you don't let me in, I'm going to have to assume it's not you in there. And if it's not you, it's a trespasser, so I'll have to call the police."

I closed my eyes, counting to three. Such a damn idiot. The best way to get yourself shot was to *inform* a possible criminal that you were going to report him. How had he survived all these years without me around to beat some sense into him?

Oh. Right. With his pretty *blond* wife.

Mary Walker—no, Mary *Holland*.

"All right." He looked the door up and down before stepping back. I hoped he wasn't about to kick it down. The damn thing wouldn't stand a chance. "Suit yourself." I saw him fish his phone out of his pocket.

Fricking Jeremy Holland. Pressing my forehead against the metal, I called out, "Call the cops and I'll shoot you myself, asshole."

He laughed, his finger hovering over the screen. "There's the Chelsea I knew and loved."

"You didn't love me," I replied coolly, resting my hand on the knob. "How's Mary?"

He didn't say anything to that. "Let me in."

"No." I shook my head, even though he couldn't see me. My heart raced and my blood rushed. Knowing he was just inches away, on the other side of this door, made me feel

more alive than I'd felt in…years. "Go home. Forget all about me."

"Not happening. Why did you lie about who you were?"

"I didn't," I said quickly. "I'm not Chelsea O'Kane anymore." I took a deep breath and focused on my story. It was imperative I convince him. "I was married, but he's gone now. I kept his last name, though. Wanted to leave my ties to the O'Kanes in the past. You know the family motto, keep looking forward."

"You got *married?* To who?" he asked, his voice hard.

"No one you knew."

"Try me." He jiggled the knob. I sucked in a breath. "Don't make me break down the pretty pink door your aunt special-ordered all those years ago because it reminded you of a fairy palace. I just want to talk."

I tightened my grip on the knob. "I'm talking to you now."

"Doesn't count." He sighed. "Open up. Prove it's you."

Rolling my eyes, I turned the lock, because there was no way he was going to leave unless I told him to, and I'd promised Paul I'd contain Jeremy. Yanking it open, I glowered at him, breathing heavily because, God, he looked good. He'd changed into a flannel shirt, which was unbuttoned and hanging loosely over a tight gray T-shirt. And those jeans—God, those *jeans*—left nothing to the imagination. "Happy now?"

His gaze raked over me, and I swore he somehow closed the distance between us without moving, because I could *feel* it. When he finally met my eyes again, there was a heat that set me on fire. "No."

"Too bad. Go home to your wife," I said, stepping back, wrapping my arms around myself, holding on tightly. Being this close to him shook me off my axis. "I'm sure she wouldn't be happy if she knew you were hanging around over here."

He entered the house, shutting himself in with me. I could feel the power radiating off him, and damned if he didn't smell exactly the same as he used to—like male, cologne, and fresh aftershave. I wanted to bury my face in his neck and breathe him in until his lips met mine like I'd fantasized about for years. Everything else faded away, but I didn't move. *That* had been a onetime deal.

After sliding the lock home, he set the food and wine down on the table—the same one that held my gun. I quickly glanced at the slightly opened drawer but focused on the real threat.

Him.

He crossed the room and grabbed my chin, clearly ignoring the *back the hell off* vibes I was throwing his way. The second his fingers touched my skin, sparks of desire laced through my blood like heroin, as he stared at me like he had every intention of picking up where we left off all those years ago. "You're blond."

"Yeah," I breathed. "So is your wife."

His grip on me tightened. "You *honestly* think I would still marry Mary after you and I slept together the night before my wedding?"

Chapter 6

JEREMY HELD HIS breath, waiting for her reply. She stared at him with wide blue eyes—eyes he'd never truly forgotten, despite how much time had passed since he'd last seen them. He scanned her face, not missing the bruising on her pale throat and underneath her eye, no matter how much makeup she'd used.

Her blond hair was...out of character.

She was beautiful, of course. Nothing would ever change that. But Chelsea as a blonde was like seeing the White House painted purple. Her lips were as plump and tempting as he remembered, and the attraction between them was as strong as ever. He'd missed her more than he'd thought possible. It felt like it was just yesterday that they had gotten drunk, kissed for the first time, and ended up naked in bed together...the night before his wedding to another woman.

That had been the shittiest thing he'd ever done.

And somehow the best, too.

"You didn't marry her?" she asked softly, swallowing

hard. She winced, like it hurt to do so. It took all his control not to pull her into his arms, hug her close, and demand she let him help her with what she was going through. "I thought we both moved on."

"How could I, after what we did?" he asked angrily. Even if it hadn't been morally wrong, he'd realized the truth that night. It had always been Chelsea.

She gripped her arms tighter, letting out a little laugh. "You loved her. What happened that night was…" She faded off and he stiffened. If she said it was a mistake, he'd show her just how much of a mistake it *wasn't*.

She sighed. "It was wonderful. But it was just a night. We both knew where your heart really belonged."

Yeah, he had thought he'd known, too. Until he kissed Chelsea and saw just how very wrong he'd been. He ran his thumb over her jawline softly. "A man who truly loves a woman isn't going to sleep with someone else the night before their wedding. My relationship with Mary was over the second you and I kissed."

"Lots of things were," she muttered, pulling free from his touch and backing up a few steps. "You shouldn't be here, Jeremy."

"Because your name change magically erased our connection?" he asked dryly.

"No." She shook her head. "Because I don't want you here. You're part of my past—a past I have no inclination to revisit. I'm moving on. Starting fresh."

"Funny, because right now, I can't think of anyone else I'd rather be with, revisiting memories." After years of searching, he'd be damned if he wanted to waste any more time playing games now that he'd finally found her again. He wasn't that same stupid kid he'd been before—the one who had been too blind to see what he wanted until it was too late.

She shook her head, biting down on her lower lip. "Well, that sucks for you, because I'm not interested. You broke my heart before. I won't let you do it again."

"You broke mine, too," he said softly—honestly—trying his best to act as unthreatening as possible. If he pushed too hard, she'd take off again. If you looked up *flight risk* in the dictionary, her picture would be next to the definition. "Why are you here? What are you running from?"

"Nothing," she said quickly.

Too quickly.

"We both know that's not true," he said, stepping closer to her. She stiffened but stood her ground as he reached out and tugged on the lock of hair that always fell into her face. He missed her normal chestnut color. "What trouble did you get into after you left?"

"The kind that's none of your business," she spat back, yanking her hair out of his grasp. "It stopped being your business when you asked Mary to marry you."

"I left her at the altar. For you."

"Not for me," Chelsea argued, shaking her head. "I was *gone.*"

"Yeah." He stopped once their toes touched. "Guess I didn't know just how *gone* you were."

"Poor you. Go home, Jeremy."

"I brought you some dinner. Something tells me you haven't eaten all day, and even if you don't want me here, you need to at least take the food."

She shook her head, biting down on her lower lip. "Stop it."

"Stop what?" he asked, cocking a brow.

"Taking care of me. This isn't just like old times. Take your food, and yourself, out of here. I'm not the same girl I was back then."

He reached out and brushed her hair out of her face. "I'm not the same boy, either. This time around, I know what I want—and I plan on getting it."

She sucked in a breath, her cheeks flushing. "Good for you. Should I clap?"

"Why are you so angry with me?"

"I'm not angry," she shot back. "I'm *busy*."

He cast a quick glance around the inn, which was in shambles and empty except for the two of them. "Clearly."

She pointed to the door.

"All right, all right. I'm going." Laughing, he turned around, opening the door and stepping outside, leaving the food on the table. The second he was on her porch, she started to swing the door shut, but his deep voice made her stop what she was doing. "I'll be seeing you soon, Chelsea."

"Don't count on it," she shot back, her voice clipped. "I'll be too busy here."

"Curious," he said, his tone soft.

She scoffed at him. "Haven't you heard what happened to the cat?"

He cocked a brow. "No."

"Curiosity killed it."

And with that, she slammed the door in his face, locking it immediately.

But underneath the anger in her voice, he heard it. The fear that caused the slight tremor in her words. Chelsea wasn't the type to be frightened, so if she was scared of something, or someone? He was going to get to the bottom of this.

Even if it did kill him.

Which it very well might.

Chapter 7

THE NEXT DAY, I slept late in an attempt to ward off the hangover pounding inside my temples, but it didn't get the memo and lingered like a bitch. Should've stuck with whiskey instead of moving to the wine Jeremy had brought over. Now I trudged up the cracked cement walkway that led to the front porch, juggling supplies from the hardware store. Pamela Mayberry ran the place now, since her father retired down to Boca Raton. Pamela peppered with me questions, trailing me around the store as I made my selections. It was only through the grace of God that I managed to carry on a polite conversation without snapping. You can take the girl out of a small town, but that small town will never forget her.

It was time to start ripping the inn apart, room by room. I'd begin with the ugly wood paneling in the living room, which would be used by guests as a common space. There would be coffee, croissants, and tea, and soft music playing as the fire roared cheerfully...

That was about as far as I'd gotten.

But it painted a pretty picture.

Smiling, I unlocked the door, almost dropping the bags in my left hand. After heaving them inside, I turned around, breathing heavily, and headed to my car for the next batch. By the time that was inside, my back ached and my palms were abraded. I started to shut the door and froze, fear shooting through my chest. There was something else on my porch, obscured by the dead potted plant to the left of the door.

Roses.

Not just any roses.

Red roses.

I glanced around the yard, looking for signs of anyone watching—*waiting*. Nothing moved except a few birds in the nearby apple tree. They chirped happily, flapping their wings, completely unaware that I was about to lose my shit. When no one jumped out to attack, I took a deep breath and bent down, grabbing the brass vase before going inside.

Slamming the door shut, I leaned against it, heart racing. I longed to throw them out without reading the note tucked among the petals, but that would be a foolish move. If there was a threat, I needed to face it head-on, not cower behind false ignorance like a scared child. That wasn't my style. I preferred using my fists for cover instead.

I glanced down at the card—and fear immediately turned to anger when I realized it was a different ghost from the past haunting me. I'd recognize that cursive *J* anywhere. That son of a bitch didn't know when to quit. Without thinking my anger through, or identifying the true cause of it, I was in my car heading for town. For *him.*

Even though I knew rationally that I shouldn't be doing this, and that I was playing right into his hands by seeking him out, it didn't stop me. When it came to Jeremy, I wasn't rational.

Which was why he was such a danger to me.

I couldn't afford to mess up right now.

Angrily, I aimed for the run-down motel off Main Street, which was the only lodging in town. I saw Jeremy's late model truck parked in front of the motel and I screeched into the parking lot. It was like it was meant to be—I'd found him so easily—but I refused to look too deeply into that. I wanted to give him the damn flowers back, and make sure he understood that I meant it when I said to stay away, since he seemed to think this was some kind of game.

He should know better.

I'd never been the playful type.

Pulling up next to his truck, I picked up the flowers and marched up to his door. Lifting my fist, I knocked hard enough to wake the dead. The door swung open, and there he was, wearing nothing but a pair of black sweats, which clung to certain parts of his body I tried very hard to forget about, thank you very much. The lack of a shirt only highlighted how good he looked, because good God, those abs had to have been chiseled by Michelangelo himself. There was no way those were *real*.

He'd always been fit, but now…

He was a freaking Adonis.

Damn him.

At my obvious appraisal of his body, he grinned and gripped the opposite side of the doorjamb, leaning closer. "You look good, too, Chels."

That annoying childhood nickname snapped me out of my haze of abs and pecs. Gnashing my teeth together, I ducked under his arm, barging in his room without invitation.

After all, he'd done the same thing to me.

"Please," he said dryly, closing the door behind me. "Come in."

The room was tiny, and being shut inside with *him* wearing practically *nothing* was too much. I needed that door open again…better yet, I needed to get the hell out of here. Away from him. "I'm not staying. Keep your stupid flowers and stop showing up at my place. I don't need you coming by, scaring the shit out of me—"

"Scaring you?" He raised a brow, crossing his arms. "Why the hell would flowers on your porch *scare* you?"

I lifted my chin, knowing I'd said too much and cursing myself because of it. When would I learn that less was more, especially when it came to Jeremy Holland? "When will you realize all I want is for you to stay away—"

"—from you." He walked across the room, not stopping until he was directly in front of me, in my personal space, doing the very *opposite* of staying away from me. "I know. I heard you. When will *you* realize I don't give a damn what you want, because I know that you're hiding something, and I'll keep asking questions until I get some answers?"

I sucked in a deep breath, watching him closely, my chest rising and falling way too rapidly. He always could read me like an open book, and clearly he hadn't lost that skill during our years apart. I needed to do something to throw him off balance.

So I did the most unpredictable thing I could think of.

I kissed him.

Chapter 8

THE SECOND OUR lips touched, I knew I'd made a big mistake. *Huge*. It came second only to running away to Miami to chase after a new life. And look where *that* had gotten me.

He gripped my shirt at the small of my back, taking over the kiss without any hesitation. His lips moved over mine, claiming me, and he moved my body so I was trapped between him and the dirty wall. There was no escape, which is the first thing I should have been focused on, but instead…

All I could think was *more*.

More tongue. More hands. More heat. More *everything*.

He lifted me up as if I weighed nothing and edged between my legs, pressing his hardness against me. I'd only felt him like this against me once before, and yet it was like my body had never forgotten just how right he felt.

Growling, he slipped his tongue between my lips. The second his touched mine, I gasped into his mouth, curling my fingers over his impossibly hard biceps. For the first time since leaving Miami, I felt like I wasn't lost. For the first time…

I felt safe.

And it was all Jeremy's fault.

I pushed at his shoulders, inhaling deeply, and turned my head to the side so he couldn't claim my lips with his own again. He was stealing the air right out of my lungs. The room was spinning, and his muscles were pressed against me, and I wanted more of him. *Oh, my God, I couldn't breathe when he was touching me.*

Sliding his hand under my butt, he thrust against me, his sweatpants and my leggings creating only a thin barrier between the two of us. Part of me wished they were gone, and the other part knew if they were, nothing would stop us from having sex right here, in his drab motel room.

"You taste so damn good," he mumbled, nibbling my ear.

I shivered, digging my nails into him. Warning bells went off in my head. I knew I had to put a stop to this before things went too far. The whole reason for this ill-advised kiss was to throw *him* off balance.

But, God help me, he didn't seem to be falling victim to my master plan.

Not even a little.

Instead, he was acting like he'd been waiting ten years for this to happen…just like I had. I skimmed my fingers down his arms, exploring his muscles as I went. Relearning the way he felt, pressed up against me. He still felt like Jeremy, but at the same time, it was like he was an entirely different man. I wasn't sure if I could handle the emotions coursing through me, but I knew one thing.

If we kept doing this…

I'd regret it.

Shaking my head, I pushed at his shoulders again, a moan escaping me as he brushed the sides of his thumbs across my nipples roughly. "We can't—oh *God*."

"Yes. We can," he rasped in reply. "We really can."

He claimed my mouth again, his hand dipping in between our bodies. The second he ran his fingers over me, I knew my defenses were gone. His tongue brushed against mine, and I clung to him, some small part of me never wanting to let go. The feeling was so familiar that it was like putting on a sweatshirt you hadn't worn in years.

It just *fit*.

Pleasure built in my stomach, spreading slowly over my body, and I rolled my hips against his fingers, and his erection. He put me down and ran a hand across my nipples, squeezing them as his other hand moved over me, and with an embarrassing quickness…

I came.

Hard.

His mouth tore free, and he dropped his forehead to rest against mine with a ragged moan. "Jesus, Chels. That was the hottest orgasm." He slipped his hand under my butt again, palming it, and lifted me. "I want more."

He sought my mouth, but I turned away at the last second, panting. "No."

"No?" He asked in surprise. "Seriously?" I pushed at his shoulders and he immediately set me down, nostrils flaring as he stepped back. "All right. I get it."

"This never should have happened. We had one night and that's it. It's done," I said, still trembling. "Finished."

"I don't know about you," he said slowly, dragging a hand through his hair, which made it stand up in a sexy, *GQ* model way. "But when I'm done with someone, I don't kiss them like I'm going to die if I don't fuck them in the next five minutes."

My cheeks heated, and I backpedaled—which was stupid, because we both knew exactly what had happened here. Panicked, I said, "I only kissed you because I thought it would scare you off."

"Why the hell would you think that?"

"Because it scares *me*." I wrapped my arms around myself. "I've spent the last few years forging a new path, doing what I want to do, and playing by *my* rules, not my father's. But after two days back here, I'm kissing you like nothing's changed at all."

He reached out hesitantly, brushing my hair behind my ear. "And that's a bad thing?"

"Yes. I'm no good for you and never have been."

Shaking his head, he pressed his mouth into a thin, hard line. "I disagree."

"That's because you always look for the good in people. Sooner or later, you'll realize there's none in me." I slid away from him, avoiding his eyes. If I looked at them, I'd get lost in their green depths, and I'd end up right back in his arms—endangering him. "Don't bring me flowers again. I don't like them."

"Why not?" he asked softly.

"My ex used to give them to me, as an apology, after he…" I broke off, refusing to say any more. It was enough. It was more than enough. "They just—they hold a different meaning for me now. Don't give them to me again."

Something crossed his eyes—rage, maybe—and he stepped closer. "I'm sorry."

I opened the door, grabbed my purse off the floor, and swallowed hard. "Stay away from me, Jeremy."

Far, far away.

Chapter 9

LATER THAT NIGHT, I was on a ladder, shoving a pry bar between the last of the wood paneling in the living room, when headlights hit my window. I sighed and shoved harder, successfully knocking down a portion of the dated wood, sending a puff of dust flying through the air in the process. I let out an exasperated breath, because I had no doubt who had just pulled into my driveway.

It had to be Jeremy.

Clearly, my warning to stay away hadn't taken.

I hopped off the ladder and removed my dust mask, heading for the door. I grabbed the bottle of whiskey off the upside-down bucket and uncapped it, swallowing a mouthful before setting it back down. My body still hummed from the orgasm he'd given me. Even though I wanted him to stay away from me and the danger surrounding me, my traitorous heart sped up at the thought of seeing him.

No matter how logically I looked at the situation, one

thing wouldn't change: My body remembered Jeremy Holland, and it wanted more of his touch.

Much more.

A girl could only save a guy from herself so many times before she stopped trying.

Being a good person didn't come naturally to me, and resisting temptation wasn't my strong suit. Eventually, I'd stop pushing him away.

And then he'd be in as much danger as I was.

Footsteps sounded on the porch as I swung the door open. "You just can't take no for an—" I broke off, the words choking me, because it wasn't Jeremy on my doorstep this time.

It was a cop.

Oh, shit. They *knew*. They found me.

"Chelsea Adams?"

"Wh—?" I blinked. Chelsea Adams…? *Paul.* He'd come through. "Y-yes?"

"I'm Officer North. I'm afraid your brother has been attacked." He removed his hat. "He told an officer you're his sister, and his emergency contact."

Paul. Oh God.

Paul was the only family I had left who wasn't behind bars, and I couldn't lose him. "What happened? Where is he?"

"He was jumped outside his office, on his way to come see you." The officer fiddled with his hat, as if unsure where to look or how to act around me. "He's in pretty bad shape, but he should recover. I can take you to him, miss, and the doctors can tell you more."

"I'll drive myself," I said quickly, reaching for my keys.

"Ma'am?" He leaned in, locking eyes with me. I stiffened, because I didn't need him all up in my face. "I can smell the whiskey from here. I think it's best I drive."

My cheeks flushed and I nodded, ducking my head down. In my worry, I'd completely forgotten about that. That wasn't like me. Then again, I'd done a lot of uncharacteristic things these past few days...my behavior with Jeremy was just the most recent example. "Right. Thank you."

The ride in the cop car was filled with awkward silence. For a moment I reveled in the novelty of riding in the front for a change. Then I started quietly panicking. Paul had just been attacked, and the timing was a coincidence, right? My brother had his fair share of enemies. I shouldn't jump to the conclusion that this was the work of the people after me.

But when I walked in the room and saw Paul lying in the hospital bed, I knew. His eyes were nearly swollen shut, and parts of his head were shaved, with thick bandages covering wounds. A thin white blanket concealed most of his body, but I could see that both of Paul's thumbs were splinted. I knew what that meant.

They were here.

Chapter 10

JEREMY PUSHED THROUGH the doors of the hospital, his heart racing as he dodged an old guy in a wheelchair. Nurses in colorful scrubs walked the halls, some clearly at the beginning of their shift, others obviously at the end. One of them, someone he vaguely recognized from high school, smiled at him as she passed, so he nodded back politely. People sat in those horrible plastic chairs in cramped waiting rooms, waiting to find out if they were losing someone they loved today.

He hated hospitals.

They reeked of desperation and death.

When he'd heard of the attack on Paul, his stomach had sunk. This wasn't supposed to be *happening,* damn it. He pushed the elevator button harder than necessary, tapping his fingers on his thigh impatiently. *"Come on,"* he growled.

He needed to see her in one piece.

With his own eyes.

The second the doors started to open, he slipped

through the crack, hitting the button for the third floor before anyone could join him. Paul had already been admitted, and word was that he'd be in the hospital for a good couple of weeks.

Paul had been beaten and tortured.

It was a miracle he was still alive.

The only reason Paul was still breathing: He was a message. A warning. One intended for his sister, and one *Jeremy* intended to take very seriously.

The doors to the elevator opened and he took a left, heading toward Paul's room. They hadn't spoken much over the years, but Jeremy had kept tabs on him. As he approached the room he slowed, walking lightly when he heard the sound of Chelsea's voice. He stopped just short of the door, where he could see them without being seen.

She spoke again and her voice washed over him like the first warm spring rain after a long, cold winter. Creeping closer, he stole a quick peek. She sat beside Paul, resting her hand on his arm gently, talking so quietly he had to struggle to hear her words. He was taken back to a time when he'd gotten his appendix out and she hadn't left his side as he recovered. Why hadn't he understood what she meant to him back then? How could he have been such a fool to lose her?

History wouldn't repeat itself this time.

"...and that's why you were attacked tonight. They're trying to flush me out."

"Shit, Chels," Paul growled.

Jeremy couldn't see her face, but her shoulders were drooped, and her head was as low as her voice. "I'm sorry. I never intended for this to happen, for you to get dragged into my fight. If I'd known they would do this…"

"I know." Paul stared at her, his bruised face looking like a sick artistic interpretation of a face rather than the real thing. "How are we going to get out of this mess?"

"There's no we, just me—" She stopped midsentence, stiffening. He held his breath. Something told him she'd discovered his presence. Or rather, sensed *someone* standing there, listening. Now she would clam up. "How did they get the drop on you?"

"What? Why—" Paul stared at her, then nodded once, glancing toward the door. I stepped back quickly, heart racing. Damn them and their silent communication. "I was leaving the DMV—" He broke off, wincing. "They came out of nowhere."

She nodded, smoothing his hair out of his face tenderly. "Criminals are good at that."

Footsteps approached, so Jeremy slid into the empty room next to Paul's, holding his breath. After a moment, the door to Paul's room shut, and he heard Chelsea say, "They're gone."

Jeremy pressed his ear to the thin wall.

"Assholes," Paul said. "How did you get mixed up with those guys anyway?"

"It's not like I meant to," she practically whispered.

"They were trying to find out if I knew where you were. I told them the truth, that we hadn't talked in years. That last I heard, you were some kind of hotshot lawyer down in Miami. I think they bought it, but you should leave, Chels. They might have someone watching the hospital."

"Shit," Chelsea said after a long pause. Jeremy could picture her sitting there, covering her face, looking exhausted as hell.

"Yeah. 'Shit' is right. The cartels don't mess around. And with what you did, they might never stop looking."

She sighed loud enough for Jeremy to hear it through the wall. "I did what I had to do, Paul. But you know what, it doesn't matter. You're right, I need to leave. Find someplace else to hide out."

Anger rushed through Jeremy's veins and he balled his hands at his sides. No. *Hell, no.* He didn't come back from Bangor for her only to watch her skip town.

She was right where he needed her to be.

Chapter 11

AFTER PAUL DRIFTED off into a morphine-induced sleep, I sat by the bed in the white room with fluorescent lights overhead, watching over him with dry, weary eyes. This was on *me*. I had assumed they would be too busy dealing with the mess I'd left behind to chase after me already. Paul had paid the price for my mistake. It was my duty to make sure it didn't happen again.

At least three people had stopped by to check on him, so news was traveling fast. After the third drop-in, I requested that no one else be allowed in, so Paul could rest.

"Chels?" Jeremy said from behind me.

I stiffened, closed my eyes, and prayed for the patience the good Lord had never given me. "How many times do I have to tell you to *leave me alone* before you finally listen?"

"Is he okay?" he asked me, coming into the room and completely ignoring my words…as usual. Sometimes I wondered if he even heard them. "What happened?"

"Some punks jumped him outside his office," I said

quickly, sticking close enough to the truth. While I thought I was an excellent liar, Jeremy did always have an uncanny knack for knowing when I was stretching the truth. "It wasn't enough to just mug him, they had to beat him, too. Assholes."

Jeremy came up beside me, staring at Paul with a furrowed brow. His hands were in his pockets, and his jaw was hard. "Some street kids took the time to break his thumbs?"

"Yeah." I gripped my knees, staring at my brother's hands. Bile rose in my throat, but I swallowed it back. Now wasn't the time or the place to lose it. "Sick, right?"

His mouth pressed into a thin, tight line. "Unbelievable." After a few moments, he let out a long breath and put his hand on my shoulder. "Let me take you home."

"I can manage on my own."

"That wasn't a question. You're exhausted, and sitting here worrying isn't going to help Paul. You need to rest."

"No." I pulled free, my heart racing and my skin burning where Jeremy had touched me. His hand stayed open, palm up and empty between us. "I need to make sure they don't come back."

"Why would a bunch of 'punks' go to all the trouble of sneaking into a hospital to attack Paul again?" he asked, his perfect brown brow arching. I hated when he did that. "I feel there's something you're not telling me. Am I right?"

"Of course you'd think that," I muttered, knowing I was

skating on the edge of giving him information he didn't need to know. "No. I'm just being paranoid. I'm worried about my brother."

"He has a police guard." He pointed out the door and I looked. Sure enough, there was a uniform outside his door. Weird. Wouldn't Paul love to know that law enforcement was lurking? The officer waved at me and I blinked at him before I recognized him. His name was...uh...Harry? No, *Larry*. He'd asked me to prom. I'd gone with Jeremy. I should've gone with Larry instead. "Paul will be fine on his own tonight. I want to make sure you're okay."

I crossed my arms, forcing my attention off the officer and back to Jeremy. Paul would have to deal with it, because having a police presence around was actually calming me. For once. "I love how you continue to think that I give a damn what you want these days."

With that, I moved closer to Paul's side, intent on ignoring Jeremy. He'd get bored watching me watch Paul sleep soon enough.

"Fine. You want to stay?" He walked over to the other chair in the room. It had been in the corner, but he dragged it right next to mine and sat. "Then we'll stay."

"Seriously?"

"Dead serious." He crossed an ankle over his knee, his heel brushing my thigh because he was so close, and leaned back as if he didn't have a worry in the whole world. "It's been ten years since we had a sleepover. And that last one was…*eye-opening,* to say the least."

I still couldn't wrap my head around the chain of events that had led us here, or what it all meant. Jeremy had chosen me over Mary. He was still choosing me. I guess, in a way, he always had. His mother had hated me because of my father, but Jeremy had never cared, always keeping his bedroom window unlocked for me whenever I needed to get away from my family. He had loved me. Of course, he apparently didn't realize he was *in* love with me until I decided enough was enough and left. Jeremy was the love of my life.

But, man, he could be such a *guy.*

"Yeah, that night was definitely eye-opening." I looked back at Paul for any signs of distress. He didn't so much as twitch. The beeping of his heart monitor remained slow and steady. "Despite, y'know, earlier, I have no interest in repeating history."

"Yeah. Me neither."

I lifted a shoulder. "Glad we're on the same page."

He leaned forward, resting a hand on my thigh. His brown hair fell on his forehead, and his piercing green eyes called for me to give him what he wanted—me. He wore a flannel shirt and a pair of ripped jeans, and his huge arms strained against the fabric of the shirt. He was so strong, so steady, and I ached to borrow some of that strength. To let him take care of me…

Again.

"You misunderstand me." Hesitantly, he reached out, cupping my cheek. "I plan on kissing you again, but I have no intention of losing you this time, Chels."

I stiffened, holding my breath, because having him here, touching me, made it oh-so-tempting to lean on him for support. Just like he wanted. Just like I *couldn't*. I wasn't that naïve girl who believed in love anymore. I lurched to my feet, shaking off his touch. If only it was as easy to lose the emotional hold he had on me. "What's it going to take to get rid of you?"

He smirked. "Easy. Let me take you home."

"Done." I grabbed my purse, checking to make sure the officer was still there. He was, and he looked a hell of a lot more alert than I felt. "And then you leave me the hell alone. Look forward, and leave the past where it belongs."

Every moment I spent with him was another moment he crept closer to my heart and threatened the new beginning I was fighting so hard for. Every moment brought danger and risk to things I wasn't willing to lose.

Like his *life*.

Chapter 12

THE SECOND JEREMY parked behind my car, I was opening the door, hopping down, and heading for the inn. I'd been too close to him for too long, and I needed space to breathe. I inserted the key into the lock with steady hands and slipped inside my sanctuary. I pushed the door shut behind me with my hip but collided with something hard. I bounced off it with a soft *oof*. This was a lovely sense of déjà vu. "What the—?"

"I want to look the place over," Jeremy said quickly, sliding inside uninvited...*again*. "After all, your brother was just attacked."

"And what will you do if you find someone?" I asked incredulously, unable to believe how incredibly hard it was for him to get the damn message. It was exhausting trying to constantly push him away—and I was all out of energy. "You're an accountant. You gonna throw a calculator at him?"

"No." He shot me a look out of the corner of his eye. "How did you know I was a CPA?"

Well, shit. I'd as good as admitted to looking him up online. I hadn't meant to be so transparent, but after Paul's attack, I was a little off my game. "Paul mentioned it once, I think. Or maybe it was Dad."

He lifted a brow. "You visited him in jail?"

Nope. Dad got locked up with a six-year sentence for breaking and entering. If he was lucky, he'd be out next year. But given his history, his freedom wouldn't last long. "What exactly are you going to do if you find someone?"

"Just because I'm an accountant doesn't mean I'm weak." He shot me a hard look. "Don't make the mistake of thinking I am."

I held my hands up defensively. "I'd never *dare.*"

Brushing past me, he glanced in the living room. "Damn. Did someone break in here and steal your walls?"

"Yes. They absolutely did," I said dryly, following him. "There's a real market for old wood paneling on eBay these days."

He snorted and moved into the kitchen, stepping over fallen paneling and nails. I'd have to clean it up at some point, but I wouldn't tonight. I was too tired. "Wow. I didn't know brown vinyl floors were back in."

I clenched my teeth. "Spare me your sarcastic comments. I know the inn needs a lot of work. Like I said yesterday, *I'm busy.* I wasn't making that up."

He glanced over his shoulder, saying nothing at all—and yet somehow saying everything at the same time. As he moved into the pantry, glancing at the bare shelves, he flicked the light on in the kitchen. It flickered, then turned fully on with a pop. "Electrical issues. Probably old knob-and-tube wiring. It'll all have to be updated to pass inspection."

I wrapped my arms around myself. "Thanks, Captain Obvious."

He grabbed a pillow off the couch on the way, holding it in front of himself like a shield and shooting me a charming grin. "I'll bring this in case anyone attacks. You know how to do wiring?" he asked, heading to the stairs.

I rolled my eyes. "Nope."

"I do," he called over his shoulder.

"Congrats?" I followed him up the stairs, trying not to stare at his butt. I failed, with a capital *F*. "Want a cookie?"

"Sure. I love cookies." He rounded the corner. "I did the wiring at Dad's place, you know. I learned a few tricks fixing up his old place before he sold it."

"How is he?"

"Dead." He flicked on the hallway light, glancing at me briefly. Shadows covered his eyes—or was it the pain from his loss? "Died two years ago. Mom shortly after."

Well, damn. I hadn't seen that on his Facebook page. Despite his parents' feelings about me, they'd been good people. They never knew about my private entrance— Jeremy's window—but they'd invited me to dinner more often than not. Jeremy wasn't allowed near my place, but I preferred his house anyway. His mother always had fresh-baked goodies on the counter, like Betty Crocker. If Betty could also shoot a deer with a rifle at a hundred yards. Mrs. Holland had been a woman of many talents. "I'm sorry. I didn't know."

"I miss them every day," he said simply. He opened the next door, glancing into the Blue Room. Or the room that would be blue, anyway, once I was done with it. Right now, it was covered in faded, peeling floral wallpaper. "You need to paint in here. Maybe something pale. Like…light blue, since it faces the ocean. That would remind your guests of the nearby beach."

I stiffened, my heart picking up speed. We used to joke that we shared a brain, because we always came up with the same ideas at the same time. Years apart and yet it was like no time had passed at all. I gestured to the cans of blue paint in the corner of the room. "That's the plan."

We studied each other. Our connection hadn't died, no matter the distance between us. It would be so easy to fall back into "us," to resume our relationship as if nothing had changed, but I couldn't. I needed to focus on the inn, on making it the warm and welcoming place I knew it would be—not on Jeremy.

He went through all the rooms, stopping when he reached mine. Slowly, he pushed the door open, turning the light on. He strode in, glancing under the bed for hidden monsters, the way he had in all the other rooms. My monsters didn't hide under beds. I leaned on the wall, watching him check my closet. Having him here was…nice. All the more reason to make him go.

As he walked away from my closet, he tossed the pillow on my bed. "I could stay here. Help you fix the place up. I'm handy."

"No, thanks," I said, shutting that idea down immediately, mostly because it made my heart soar and my legs go a little weak. The idea of having Jeremy under the same roof as me, helping me transform this place…it wasn't exactly a *bad* one. "I don't take charity."

He flexed his jaw. "It's not charity. I'm paying an arm and a leg to stay at that cheap-ass motel because it's the only lodging in town. Fixing up the inn gives people like me options. This place is much nicer, and you can play the whole 'short walk to the beach' angle that the motel could never claim. It's the perfect small-town getaway. You could host honeymooners—any couple, really, looking for a romantic weekend. Maybe even weddings."

"That's the plan," I repeated. "You think I didn't think of that?"

"I know you did. But the thing is, being here, looking at the rooms?" He smiled, locking eyes with me. "I can *feel* it. I can feel the things this place could be, what it could offer people. And, damn it, Chels, I want to be a part of it. I want to help you rebuild."

I didn't say anything. Mostly, because all I could think

of saying was *yes*. But I couldn't. He'd suck me back into his world of goodness and I wasn't naïve enough to think that world existed anymore.

"Let me help you open this place up sooner. I'll be in town for a week, so let me lend you a hand while I still can." He gestured toward the hallway, walking across the room. My bedroom felt a million times smaller with him in it. I stared at him as he crept closer, one step at a time. When he was directly in front of me, I crossed my arms in front of me defensively. "I think it's really special what you're doing here, rebuilding the inn. Let me be a part of it. Of you." He blinked. "That came out wrong. I meant...screw it."

And then, without warning, he cupped my cheek. Before I could exhale, he was kissing me, and I was clinging to him, and his hands were everywhere. I couldn't think of any other place I'd want Jeremy to be than *here*. I wanted him with me, fixing up the inn, building a future that was so real that I could feel it, too. He slid his hand up my shirt, cupping my breast, and claimed my mouth with no mercy and no hint of hesitation.

He just...took.

And I gave. *Willingly*.

Arching my back, I dug my nails into his shoulders, letting out a soft moan. His phone rang, and he stiffened, his lips going hard against mine before he pulled back. "Shit."

I shoved at his shoulders. "If you didn't want to kiss me, then you shouldn't have—"

"It's not that. I just didn't want to push you when you were vulnerable," he said, pulling away from me and ignoring his ringing phone. "I meant what I said, though. Can I help you?"

Swallowing, I stared at him, knowing I was in over my head. There's only so much you can learn from construction how-to books and YouTube. Besides, no matter how much I pushed Jeremy away, he kept showing up, so I might as well save my energy for more important things...like staying *alive*. "If you're going to help, you can stay here for free as payment."

"Deal." His grin lit up the room better than any flickering light ever could. "You won't regret this."

That might be true, but one way or another...*he* would.

It was only a matter of time.

Chapter 13

THE NEXT MORNING, Jeremy was under the sink with dirty water dripping on his face and the edge of the cabinet digging into his back. The TV was on in the living room and he could just barely make out what the news anchor was saying. He'd heard the telltale dripping under the sink when he came down to the kitchen to make coffee, and he figured that there was no time like the present to start earning his keep. He intended to make sure Chelsea had no valid reason for kicking him out, since he was exactly where he wanted to be. Sooner or later, she would trust him again and tell him the truth she was trying so hard to hide. Footsteps approached, and he torqued the wrench harder. "Morning, Chels."

The footsteps stopped at his side. Though he couldn't see her, he could easily picture her frowning down at him, arms crossed. "What are you doing under there?"

"Admiring the old lead pipes."

"Ha-ha," she muttered. "So funny."

He pushed out from under the sink, swiping his forearm over his forehead as he eyed her. She wore a loose pink shirt and a pair of leggings that hugged her curves. "There was a leak in the pipes where they joined."

She frowned, and he glanced down at her soft lips. "Since when?"

"I don't know. I just got here, but judging from the damp wood under me, I'd say a long time. But it's fixed now." As Jeremy stood, Chelsea's eyes drifted down his shirtless torso. "Neighbors brought pie, casserole, and those."

She eyed the red roses he'd deliberately thrown away. "And questions about Paul?"

"Of course." He grabbed the mug off the counter, filled it with coffee, and handed it to her. "Still like it black?"

"Yeah." She took the mug and her fingers brushed his. It was just like old times, when he used to bring her coffee every day before class, since they had gone to the same college. She could've gone away to school, but when he got a baseball scholarship for the state university, she followed him there. As her fingers left his skin, he swallowed hard. Just that simple touch was enough to make him want to pull her in his arms and kiss away the worry he could see in her eyes. "Some things never change."

"Guess not."

She set the coffee down, leaned on the old maple cabinets, and stared at him. Chelsea had a way of staring at a guy that made it feel like she saw all the way to the bottom of his soul. It was enlightening and scary all at once. "Why didn't you marry Mary? After all those years together, telling me that she was the love of your life, you just…left her behind."

"I was wrong. I didn't love her," he said simply. "Why'd you marry that guy?" He was curious to see what she'd say, since they both knew she'd never been married. "I gather from what you've let slip that he was a dick."

"I don't know. I keep asking myself that question." She tapped her fingers on the counter. "Why did you take the boring desk job?"

"I was looking for something different. A change." He shrugged. "Why'd you run away?"

"Same reason. I didn't want to be the girl who was in love with a boy who didn't love her back. And I definitely didn't want to be known only as Johnny O'Kane's daughter anymore."

Her words touched him. He'd always told her that she could be more than her family. He couldn't help but feel that even though she'd done her best to leave him in the past, there was still a small chance he'd be in her future. "I always loved you. I just didn't know the truth until it was too late. After I canceled the wedding, I went down a dark hole. Drank too much. Slept too little. Was angry at the world."

She turned away. "Yeah. I know the feeling all too well."

"Fixing up this place with you, I think it'll be good." He glanced around the kitchen, seeing it as it could be, not the cracked wood on the cabinets and the peeling wallpaper. "For both of us. What do you think of white cabinets?"

"*Love* them." She came alive at the mention of the renovations, no longer looking as if she'd rather be somewhere else. "I think they'll brighten this place up, especially if we do a blue-and-white backsplash, too. I'd like to have pastries and coffee in the living room, over there, for guests who don't want room service. Or they could eat in the formal dining room with the other guests, and I could have a buffet-style breakfast in here."

"That's a great idea." He rubbed his chin. "You seem pretty experienced at this stuff. Where have you been? I heard you were down in Florida."

"I was," she said hesitantly.

"Were you in hotel management down there?"

Just like that, the excitement died in her eyes. "No."

"So what did you do?"

Chelsea stiffened the second he pried into her past. It was infuriating. What would it take to get her to open up to him? "I was an assistant district attorney."

"And now you're back here...fixing up inns?" He worked his jaw. "It takes guts to walk away from that degree, if you ask me. Why leave all that?"

"I didn't." Leaving her coffee untouched on the counter, she bumped shoulders with him as she started to leave the room. *Escape* was more like it. "I'm going on a few errands. Won't be back till later tonight."

"We'll continue this conversation later," he called out.

She didn't reply. Just banged the front door shut behind her.

Jeremy trailed after her, watching her from the window as she got in her beater. He wanted to tag along to keep her safe, but he knew he'd be pushing his luck. He'd already wormed his way into her home. If he pushed any harder, she'd snap. If this was going to work, he needed to stay close to her.

"And in other news, a district attorney is the latest victim of increased gun violence in Miami. Dental records have confirmed that Richard Seville, who was a popular candidate for the mayoral office in Miami due to his generosity with the people of the city and his conservative political leanings, has been murdered. Authorities say someone broke into his home late Monday night, killing him. Police are looking for help to identify and locate the woman seen fleeing the scene, who is described as…"

He stopped listening, pulling out his phone and quickly dialing. "The story went national," he said, as soon as the other person picked up. "We need to move faster."

Chapter 14

I'D NEARLY DRIVEN into a tree when I got Paul's text. CNN's covering it. I still remembered what a comfort my brother had been to me as I'd spilled all my dirty secrets. It was bad enough that Paul had put two and two together with the little bit I'd told him, but what if Jeremy did, too? I guess I had let myself fall into a false sense of security as the days ticked by with no repercussions. Now I had a brother in the hospital and the media shining a spotlight on things.

I pulled over to check out the link Paul had texted. I scanned the article quickly and breathed a sigh of relief, dropping my phone back onto my lap. They didn't seem to have too many details. It said that Richard was shot in his home and that his death was further proof we were losing the War on Drugs. No duh.

The situation clearly called for junk food, so I swung by Ollie's Diner to pick some up for me and Paul. In his hospital room, we talked about the new development, but that only led to circular arguments. There was nowhere to go with this mess.

A day later, I sat in my car again, trying to muster the courage to head into the inn. Jeremy was painting in the living room and I had a bag of supplies on the passenger seat. I had to admit, once Jeremy had started pitching in, a lot more progress had been made on the renovations. I flitted from project to project, doing whatever caught my attention at that moment, but Jeremy always liked to finish what he started.

I couldn't help but compare him to Richard. Richard never let me "flit around." He was a massive control freak and needed to oversee everything from start to finish. That included people. We had met at the holiday party, back when I first started at the DA's office. He was already a rising star. I thought we'd been swept away—that our relationship was like something out of a romance novel—whereas he saw a puppet he could manipulate.

Little did he know that there ain't no strings on me.

My reverie was interrupted by a woodpecker doing its thing in the trees. I should run again. I knew I should, but…I didn't really want to. Maybe I needed to be more like that woodpecker and just keep banging away until I got what I wanted. Maybe it was time to stand my ground and fight. Turning my head, I looked at my inn, the place I wanted to make my sanctuary. Over the past few days,

Jeremy and I had bonded over our plans to renovate, and for once, things felt *normal*. I was dreaming of a future like any other average person.

And then it got blown apart by CNN.

All the blinds were pulled up in the living room, and I could see Jeremy standing on a ladder, painting the walls that I'd taped the other night. He'd sanded them yesterday, and now the plaster was getting new life under his roller with the paint I'd carefully picked out. My dreams were coming to life, but at any moment, they'd die in front of me.

God, could I be any more melodramatic?

Shaking my head, I cut the moping, straightening my spine. I wouldn't be *that* girl. I would be the girl who fought. Look at what I'd done to get here. If the cartels wanted a fight? Well, then, I'd give them a fight on *my* turf. If they wanted to come at me, they'd have to do it in the broad light of day. No more shadows for me. That part of my life was over. It *had* to be. I was Chelsea…Adams.

And I wasn't going *anywhere*.

Besides, if they knew where I was, I'd be dead already. They were obviously using the cops to try to flush me out, so I had time to come up with a game plan. My aim was to win. I grabbed the supplies out of the backseat and trudged up to the front door. Rock music blared out the open windows, and Jeremy sang along loudly and out of tune. Smiling, I glanced up at the old inn and saw home.

And Jeremy was undeniably a part of that picture,

whether I liked it or not. I wasn't sure if I did yet. But that was okay. For once, I was okay with being unsure. Waiting to see how things worked out between the two of us should have scared me, but with danger lurking...yeah, it didn't. It was freeing to not give a damn anymore. Opening the door, I set the bags down. Jeremy's biceps flexed and hardened as he stroked the roller up the wall, set on making my dreams a reality. I took a second to admire the view, then called out, "I'm home."

"Did you get everything?"

"Yup." I came into the room, studying his workmanship. It was flawless. Excitement built inside me and I smiled. "That light peach is even prettier on the walls than it was on the card."

"It really brightens up the place," he agreed, grinning. "Did you decide whether you want the fireplace painted?"

"Yep." I pointed to the cans of paint at my feet. "Antique white won."

He nodded. "Good choice."

"Yeah. Paul suggested it." I tucked my hair behind my ear. "He'll be coming to live here, with us, once he's out next week, by the way. Once he's healed, he can help us out with renovations."

"Do you think that's—?" He gave the wall one more stroke before turning around mid-sentence. As he did, his sleeve brushed the wet wall. "Well, shit."

I laughed, but cut it off quickly when he shot me a

narrow-eyed look. Forcing a straight face, I asked, "Do I think it's what?"

"Funny?" he asked, ripping his shirt over his head and hopping off the ladder effortlessly. He landed on both feet, dropping the shirt as his feet touched. I gulped down air, because, God, those *abs*. He stalked toward me, his eyes narrow.

I forced myself to stand my ground, even though I wanted to flee for my life. The cartel didn't send me running, but give me a shirtless Jeremy and I was a goner. "Yes?"

That brow shot up, and he took another step toward me. "Is that a question?"

"No." I lifted my chin. "I think it's funny you got paint on you, without a doubt."

Reaching out, he rested a tender hand on my shoulder, skimming his hand over the bare skin of my shoulder by my tank top straps. "Good. I'd hate to make you uncertain about anything when it comes to me. I know what I want from you, and I want you to feel the same certainty I do."

He lowered his face to mine, his eyes seductive.

I closed my eyes, breath held, ready to be kissed, and then he…

Ran the paint roller down my face.

Fricking Jeremy Holland.

Chapter 15

I GASPED, STUMBLING back with wide eyes, my mouth parted in surprise, and trying my best to act as if he'd taken me off guard by painting me instead of kissing me. Well, I mean, he *had*. But I wasn't so off balance that I couldn't start plotting my revenge. Dad had taught me a few tricks, and Jeremy wouldn't see me coming till it was too late. "I can't believe you just did that," I shrieked, lurching backward until I bumped into something.

He started laughing hysterically, bending over, taking his attention off me. *Jackpot.* "You…should…see…your… *face.*"

"I can't," I answered, creeping closer and closing my fist around my target. His laughter washed over me like a million lights in a gloomy basement. "But I can see yours."

He glanced up just in time for me to swipe the paintbrush I'd grabbed from the can across his entire face—and into some of his hair. He jumped back, but not quickly enough. He blinked at me, his eyes standing out comically against the light-peach paint, and his lips bright pink in contrast. I burst into laughter, pointing at him. "Oh my God. If I look anything like that, then—*agh!*"

I hit the floor, his arms cradling me so I didn't get hurt. The second we settled, he caught my arms over my head, trapping my weapon, leaving me defenseless with Jeremy Holland between my thighs. As he struggled to hold both my wrists with one hand, he lifted the roller threateningly. "Oh, so you want to play dirty?"

"You started it," I accused, arching my back, trying to throw him off. It did nothing besides let him settle in between my legs more firmly. I gasped when he rolled his hips, teasing me with his hardness. "*Now* who's playing dirty?" I said.

"Baby, you have no idea how dirty I can get," he murmured, dropping the roller and cupping my cheek. Tilting my chin up, he stared down into my eyes, his grip tightening on me. "But I'm willing to show you, if you'd like."

"Yes," I breathed, anticipation making my nerves tingle. "God, yes."

The breath I'd been holding burst out at the exact moment his lips touched mine, making everything seem right in the world again. He was hesitant at first, probably giving me a chance to change my mind, but when I strained to get closer, he claimed me fully. It was as if I'd been walking a labyrinth for the last eight years, and the second he was holding me, *kissing* me, the maze went straight, and suddenly I knew exactly where I was going and why.

He didn't let go of my wrists, but ran his thumb over my pulse gently as his tongue swept inside my mouth. He tasted like beer and Jeremy, a combination I missed more than I cared to admit. I slid my hand over his lower back, pressing closer to him as I curled a leg around him, locking him in place. There was no doubt. No fear. Okay, that was a lie. The way he made me feel scared the hell out of me. But even so?

It just felt *right*.

Skimming his hand down my sides, he deepened the kiss, stealing the last bit of coherent thought from my mind until all I could focus on was getting him naked and buried inside me. I needed Jeremy with a passion that burned me, that changed me, and there was no stopping now that we'd begun again.

I tugged at his shirt, moaning and writhing beneath him impatiently. Tearing my mouth free of his, I sucked in a breath, the room spinning around us. "I need you. *Now*."

He slid his hand under my butt, nodding, pressing his forehead to mine. "You have me. You always have." He caught my mouth again and rocked his erection against me, sending pleasure through my veins. I pushed closer, desperate for the release only he could give me, and dug my nails into my palms, tugging for him to free my wrists.

He let go immediately, like he'd just been reminded he

had been holding them, and stopped kissing me. Instead of keeping his lips on mine, he brought them down my body, one torturous inch at a time. My jaw. My throat. Directly over my pulse. My collarbone. The top of my breast. The lower he went, the faster my heart raced, and it got so loud, I swore he heard it, too.

So loud, I could feel the glass of the window above shattering over us, slicing my skin with its jagged edges—wait, what?

Jeremy threw himself over my body, completely shielding me, and it was then—oh God, it was *then*—that I realized the pounding I'd heard wasn't my heartbeat. It had been bullets, breaking windows, and implanting themselves in the freshly painted plaster. And those bullets were still coming, showing no sign of stopping anytime soon. Jeremy cursed, covering my body even more, pressing me down into the floor so hard that I couldn't breathe.

We were going to die.

Chapter 16

JEREMY GRITTED HIS teeth, growling as the bullets whizzed over his head, somehow miraculously avoiding them. One second, he'd been in heaven in Chelsea's arms, and the next, the threat of danger became all too real. He'd let his guard down, forgotten for a split second that he was supposed to be keeping her *safe,* and look what had happened. She'd almost been killed.

The second the bullets stopped, he was on his feet. They might just be pausing to reload, but he didn't give a damn. With Chelsea in danger, he wouldn't stand here waiting to find out and not fight back. "Stay down. Got it?"

She nodded, eyes wide, opening her mouth. She had small cuts on her cheeks and arms from the glass but otherwise looked fine. He didn't wait for her to speak. Instead, he took off out the front, taking the gun that she'd stowed in the table by the door. He didn't bother to look back when she gasped. There wasn't time. He had to catch those assholes who dared to shoot at his girl, damaging what she was trying to fix. Hell, he had to save her life, so she could be *his* girl, and so this place could become an inn again.

He bolted onto the porch, leaping off and raising the gun at eye level.

A dented black Cadillac screeched around the corner, out of shooting range. His finger tightened on the trigger. He ached to put a few holes in those sons of bitches, but he didn't have the shot. *"Shit."* Lowering the gun, he pulled his phone out, sent off a quick text, and headed back inside the inn.

Chelsea stood shakily, pressing a hand to her stomach. Her face was pale and she looked seconds from falling over, so he shoved the gun back in the drawer and rushed to her side, running his hands over her in case he'd somehow missed an injury besides her superficial wounds. "What's wrong?"

Shaking her head, she pressed her lips into a thin line and gripped his bicep, holding on to it tightly. She choked on a laugh. *"Everything's* wrong. Someone just shot up my home and tried to kill us."

"Yeah. They did. But they failed." Jeremy took a deep breath and pulled her into his arms, curling his hand behind her head and cradling it protectively. She was so brave and so strong that sometimes he forgot she wasn't in this line of work. Or at least she wasn't supposed to be. "I've got you, Chels. I won't let anything happen to you."

"That's sweet." She buried her face in his chest, breathing deeply, and for the first time since she came back, she leaned on him. "But it's a foolish thing to say. You have no idea what's going on."

He held her close, preparing for the worst. "So tell me."

"There's nothing to tell." She pushed off his chest, but her hands lingered. "The decisions I made, the messes I created, they're mine. I don't need anyone trying to fix them for me. If you know what's good for you, you'll stop trying. You've seen what happens when people try to help me. From here on out, I go it alone."

He caught her hand, refusing to let her go. "Tell me what you're planning to do."

"What makes you think I'm planning anything at all?" Chelsea crossed her arms defensively.

It was on the tip of his tongue to tell her the truth, but he didn't say a damn word. Sirens sounded outside. "I—"

"Shit." She pushed her hair out of her face, going even paler than before. "Someone called the cops?"

"There was a bunch of gunfire. Of course someone called the cops. Do you have a reason to hide this from them?" he asked slowly, locking eyes with her. "Is there something you want to tell me before they get here?"

"I…" She opened her mouth, closed it, and then shook her head. Disappointment hit him in the chest like a lingering bullet. "Nope. Nothing."

"Okay." Clenching his jaw, he headed for the door. "Stay in here. I'll take care of this and send them on their way."

As he walked out the door, he shut it behind him, heading for the closest car. The red-and-blue lights blinded him as Larry stepped out of the driver's seat. "What happened here, Jeremy?"

He sighed, pulling his wallet out of his pocket. Larry's gaze dipped down, then shot back up immediately. "I'll tell you everything you need to know, but then you need to get the hell out of here."

Chapter 17

WITH JEREMY OUTSIDE, handling the cops, I rubbed my hands up and down my arms as I surveyed the damage to the walls and windows. This would easily set us back a few days and a few hundred dollars. But that wasn't what really mattered. What mattered was that *they* were getting closer. Soon they'd discover the truth about Richard. It was a truth I couldn't accept, but I'd done what I needed to do to survive and get out of there alive.

If I wasn't careful, my past was going to destroy everything I loved. It was time to take care of business. Obviously, my plan to escape and fade into the sunset wasn't working out, so I needed a new one. One that wouldn't quite have a happy ending for me.

If I was going down, the least I could do was make sure no one else went down with me. I had to make sure Paul and Jeremy would be okay. There was one course of action left available to me. The door opened and I stiffened, waiting for the cops to come in and question me. Instead,

Jeremy came in alone. The flashing lights outside turned off and headlights hit the windows as the cars pulled away. "What's going on?"

"They got a lead on the shooters, headed down on Main Street." Jeremy locked the door but didn't come any closer. Just stood there. "After they investigate, they'll be back to ask questions. Probably in the morning."

I blinked. "They just…" I held my hands out, their palms facing up. "…*left?*"

"This isn't Florida," Jeremy said dryly, rubbing the back of his neck. "There are four cops in town, and there's never been a drive-by. When it happened, they sent the two on-duty cops here. When Mr. Brady, down by Route 22, called in to report some kids joyriding in a city-slicker car, they went to see if they could catch them. An off-duty officer was told to keep watch here, in case the shooters come back, but Larry—from high school, you remember—he thinks they'll catch the kids tonight."

"Good." I wrapped my arms around myself, shivering. "I thought this was supposed to be a safe town. It's why I came back."

"It is a safe town, relatively speaking." He crossed the room, pulling me into his arms. He ran his hands up and down my bare biceps, warming me the way only he could. "I don't know why this keeps happening to you guys."

"What do you mean?" I asked hesitantly, resting my cheek on his chest for a second. *Just one second.*

He shrugged, still running his hands over my arms. I melted into him more, even though I knew better than to lean on a guy like Jeremy. If I let him, he'd swoop in and try to fix all my problems, and I needed to do that all on my own. "Weird, huh? You and Paul having such a run of bad luck?"

"I guess." I swallowed. "Why did you come back?"

"To town?"

I nodded. "Yeah."

"I missed small-town life. I don't know what I was looking for when I left, but I didn't find it. The second I knocked on this door, though, and you opened it..." He pulled back, tipping my chin up gently with his hand so our eyes could meet. "I found what I've been looking for all this time. This inn, and you...it just feels right."

He stared at me silently, his eyes asking a million questions. Questions I couldn't answer. I glanced away, staring at the drawer he'd so fluidly opened earlier since it was easier than looking at him. It wasn't that I didn't trust or care about him. It was that I saw how all this was going to end, and it didn't include him and me together.

Stepping out of his reach, I felt the loss of his heat immediately. "How long have you known about the gun?"

"Since I moved in." He crossed his arms and leaned against the door. "Does the fact you're keeping that gun handy connect to your recent misfortunes?"

I lifted a shoulder. "Not really. Like you said, bad luck. Or maybe karma, coming to collect."

He laughed, but there was no warmth to it. "So you're not worried about this?"

"Aside from the fact that we now have to fix up all the damage they caused? No." I crossed the room, opening the drawer. His green eyes followed my every movement as I picked up the gun. "But I think I'll bring this up with me tonight, for safekeeping."

"I want to stay here to renovate longer than we origi-nally talked about." He rubbed the back of his neck, duck-ing his head and watching me. "I spoke to my boss. He said I can work remotely for as long as I want. You clearly need more help here than you thought—"

I stiffened. "I do not."

"Chels. Your walls are literally shot up."

My cheeks heated, and I turned my face away. The idea of him sticking around wasn't unpleasant, but shouldn't he *want* to leave? We'd just been shot at, for God's sake. I had a feeling that wasn't something an accountant was accus-tomed to. "I'm fine on my own. You need to stop worrying about me. As a matter of fact, in light of these new events, if you're gone in the morning, I totally understand."

He flexed his jaw, staring at me through narrowed eyes. "*I'm* not the one who runs away."

"Then you're an even bigger fool than I thought."

I headed up the stairs without another word, and, mira-cle of all miracles, he let me. As I walked down the hallway to my empty room, I tightened my grip on the gun more with each step. By the time I closed the door behind me, I was breathing heavily. My knuckles hurt, my throat ached, and my chest burned…but I refused to give in to the urge to cry.

Big girls don't cry. Dad's voice echoed in my head, filled with reprimand and disgust. He'd hated shows of emotion, so at a young age, I'd learned to show none. My mother had taken off pretty much the second she finished pushing, and I hadn't heard from her since. All I'd had was Dad, and Paul…and Jeremy. Leaning against the door, I took a deep breath in, exhaling it slowly. *Repeat until you regain control.*

After a few times, the burn eased and I was able to breathe…until I looked at the bed. On my pillow, bright against the white pillowcase, were four red roses. Anger choked me, and I stalked to the bed, picking them up in one swipe. A small card read: *together again.* Clearly, Jeremy hadn't listened when I'd told him to stop with the flowers.

I tossed them in the trash and slid the gun under my pillow. Sinking onto the mattress, I opened my MacBook and clicked on the email icon. I'd need all the help I could get. It wasn't every day a girl gave up everything she fought hard for to save someone else.

Especially not a girl like *me.*

Chapter 18

JEREMY WATCHED CHELSEA from across the living room as he held the white crown molding against the wall, lining it up to see what it looked like. It was going to match the fireplace perfectly. After the drive-by three days ago, they'd been on overdrive to get the living room put back together. They'd replaced the broken windows, plastered the bullet holes, and repainted. The room was coming back to life.

Chelsea hadn't been much of a talker these past few days. Instead, she'd been single-mindedly focused on finishing everything as quickly as possible. Jeremy couldn't help but think it was because she was racing against some kind of inner clock. He was losing any grip he had on her. She had a certain air that screamed defeat, but if he had anything to say about it, she'd never lose. It would help if she would just trust him and tell him what he needed to know instead of leaving him to fill in the blanks himself. He knew he could fix this with minimum damage.

Aside from the inn.

Then they could continue reconnecting. There had been a few passionate kisses here and there, but for the most part, she was still holding him at arm's length. What she didn't know was that he was scared, too. But that's when you know it's real.

When it scares the shit outta you.

"Jeremy?"

He snapped himself back to the present. "Yeah?"

"You mentioned wanting to stick around here, while working remotely. Said you wanted to live in a small town again. Right?"

He swallowed. "Right."

She stroked the brush over the mantel, leaving it a shiny antique white. Paul had been right. It complemented the peach walls perfectly. "Well...if I had to leave again for, for reasons, would you keep working on this place, bringing it back to life even if I wasn't here?"

He froze, staring at her, his heart pounding. And there it was, the confirmation that she was planning something that would result in her leaving all this work undone. "Of course, I'll do whatever you need me to do. But where are you going?"

"Nowhere." She stroked the brush again, still not looking at him. "Just hypothetically thinking out loud."

Bullshit. She was up to something. While he was honored she trusted him enough to leave the inn in his hands, he'd rather she trusted him with the goddamn truth about why she was running away... *again*. "Did the cops come by yesterday?" he asked casually.

She nodded, staring at the mantel as she ran the paintbrush over a spot she'd missed. "Yep."

"I heard the investigation into those joyriding kids didn't pan out, and they still don't know who shot at us. Did they give you any new details? Something that sparked these hypothetical thoughts you're having?"

She stiffened at that last part. "Nope. I told them that I moved here to fix up the inn, and that my place got shot up." She swiped the brush across the mantel harder. "That's all I know, so that's all I told them. End of story."

Jeremy gritted his teeth. Enough was enough already. Obviously, she trusted him enough to put him in charge of the inn. Now she needed to trust him with her secrets, too. "Really, Chels? After all this time, you still won't let me in, not even a little?"

"I don't know why you keep asking me about this. You were there! You saw everything I did. Maybe even more." She turned around, her cheeks slightly red and her lips parted. "You're turning out to be a lousy worker, more interested in gossip than actually helping. Are you going to nail those strips of molding to the wall, or are you hoping they magically attach themselves?"

He threw the wood down and held his hands out at his sides. "I don't know. You seem to believe in the impossible, as if I wouldn't remember that your voice goes up when you lie, so maybe you believe in magic, too. Or, better yet, maybe you could, I don't know, tell me the *truth*. Why do you need a caretaker for the inn? You running away again?"

For a second, just a brief fucking second, she opened her mouth, and he thought she was going to finally talk. But then she closed it, shrugged, and shot down his hopes with a single word. "Whatever."

When she turned back to the mantel, ignoring him again, something inside him snapped. He stalked across the room, rage consuming him, and spun her around by the shoulder. "Damn it! Stop *ignoring* me. I'm trying to save your ass, and you won't let me."

Her nostrils flared. "No one asked you to ride back into my life on some quest to save me. I don't need you, or any other man, trying to be my knight in shining armor. I can defeat my own dragons, thank you very much."

Suddenly she looked more alive than she had in days. So that was the way to get her talking. Piss her off. Luckily, he was good at that. He gestured to the formerly shot-up wall and said, "Looks like you suck at it."

Her cheeks flushed, and she pointed an angry finger at him. "Screw you. You think you can just come in here and the world will arrange itself to your will, that everything will be sunshine and rainbows just because you say so. Guess what? It doesn't matter if you're a good person or if you try to do the right thing, because evil will triumph over goodness every time. And I hate…I hate…." A frustrated sound escaped her, and she stomped her foot, just like she used to do when they were younger. Just like she had ten years ago, when she told him she loved him and that he was a fool for agreeing to marry someone else. "I hate *you*."

He did the same thing he had done all those years ago, when she said those same three words to him. Growling, he wrapped his arms around her, hauling her against his chest, burying his fingers in her hair and splaying the other hand across her back.

"Yeah, well, I love you. So tough shit." The second he said it, he knew he had made a huge mistake. Chelsea and feelings didn't mix, and he was going to scare her off before he had a chance to save her life. Her eyes widened and her lips parted, and he did the one thing guaranteed to shut her up.

He kissed her.

Chapter 19

I STRAINED AGAINST him, trying to get closer, knowing I should be pushing him away. He loved me, and I was only going to break his heart. When this whole thing was over and the dust had settled, he would be left alone, sad, missing me—and I didn't want that for him. He deserved more than memories. I broke the kiss off, trembling, every inch of my body begging for more. "Are you sure?"

He grabbed my hair and my shirt, nodding, not letting go. "You're the best thing that ever happened to me, and I'm not losing you again, Chels. Yes, I'm sure."

My heart twisted, and I opened my mouth to tell him he *had* to lose me again. I did trust him, but I'd already put plans in motion. The other night, after mourning the loss of the life I wouldn't get, I'd contacted the feds. I hated them even more than the cops—being an O'Kane and all, I couldn't help it. But in a few days, I'd disappear again with my brother at my side, and there would be no finding me this time.

It would be over between Jeremy and me, and he'd be better off because of it.

But the second his lips touched mine, I swallowed the words. He backed us out of the living room, his lips never leaving mine as we stumbled toward the stairs. By the time we made it to my bedroom, I was a mess of trembling need and untapped emotion—a dangerous combination. We fell back on the bed and it felt so right that it stole my breath. All the more painful that soon, I'd be losing him all over again.

Over the past few days, I'd pictured an actual life with Jeremy by my side as my accountant and jack-of-all-trades. And damn it, that life we could have shared had sounded good. Him. Me. Falling in love all over again. Turning this inn into a home for us and a sanctuary for others. It had been everything I ever wanted.

His hands roamed over my body. Down my hip, around the swells of my breasts, across my ribs. When he closed a hand over my breast, dragging the side of his thumb across my hard nipple, I gasped. Desire pooled in my belly, and I wrapped my legs around his waist. He took advantage of my open mouth, his tongue slipping inside to claim mine as he squeezed my nipple between his fingers.

We undressed each other with unsteady hands, clothes flying everywhere. By the time I was down to a thong, its matching red bra tossed on the floor, all rational thought fled my brain. I lay on the bed, breathing heavily, as he tugged his boxers down. When he stood there, naked, staring down at me as if I meant the whole world to him, I sucked in a breath.

And I didn't exhale. If I did, I'd say something stupid like how I loved him, too. I'd say he was the only man who had never lied to me.

He rolled a condom on and crawled up my body, leaving kisses in his wake. My calf. My knee. He placed a love bite on my inner thigh, then rolled my thong down my legs, his fingers burning on my skin as he went. A fire was hot within me, and there was only one way to put it out.

I spread my legs, letting my knees fall to the side. He slipped his hands under my ass, lifting me up to his mouth, and finally gave me what I wanted—his mouth on me. It was magical, and crazy, and so powerful that for a second I thought I might be dreaming this whole thing. But then his fingers dug into my skin, his teeth scraped me, and I was breathing heavily, panting, and writhing against his mouth as the pleasure rose higher and higher. I couldn't *breathe*.

After a few minutes of this perfect torture, he rolled his tongue over me, once, twice, and with mind-clearing clarity, I came hard, my whole body hardening impossibly before I collapsed, breathing heavily. He didn't stop there, like any other man would have.

Instead, he tapped my sensitive flesh, sending me soaring over the edge again, tears running down my face because it was so intense. Every nerve, every sensation, was heightened because this was Jeremy. He was the one. He'd always been the one. The only reason I'd been with Richard was because I didn't think I deserved this—I didn't deserve a guy like Jeremy. Especially after what we'd done the night before his wedding. In a way, I was punishing myself by ruining the only good thing I'd ever had in life.

I'd stayed with an abusive asshole because I let myself believe it was what I deserved. Once this was all over and I turned into state's evidence, they would take me away to my new life in protective custody, where I'd keep lowballing myself.

I would lose Jeremy all over again.

And this time, I had no one but myself to blame.

Chapter 20

JEREMY HAD WAITED for this moment way too damn long, and now that he had Chelsea in his arms, clinging to him, limbs trembling from the pleasure he'd given her, he wasn't quite sure what to do with himself. Ever since she'd left him, sex had been just that—*sex*. Meaningless. Empty. A way to fulfill a basic need, but nothing more.

With Chelsea, it was everything.

This wasn't about lust or desire.

It was a promise from him to her, a way to show her she could trust him to stick around no matter what happened, even though she seemed so damn certain he was going to somehow mess her life up again. Apparently she thought men like him couldn't handle the type of trouble she was in. Or maybe she thought he was only looking out for himself—just like her father.

So when she found out the secrets he held, she'd be pissed as hell.

Her first instinct would be to push him away. But his

first instinct would be to hold her close. Through the worst of her anger, he'd be there at her side. Eventually she'd forgive him. Years had changed nothing on his end. He'd just been waiting for her to come home when she was ready. She'd done that, and she'd brought a shitload of trouble with her.

It was his job to clean it up.

Closing his mouth over hers, he slid between her legs, groaning at the feelings of her skin on his—something he'd craved over the past ten years more than anything else in the world. She wrapped her legs around him, still trembling from the orgasms he'd already given her.

If he had it his way, he'd spend the rest of his life making her scream his name. Making her happy, because, damn it, Chelsea deserved some happiness in her life. It'd only been recently that he'd finally discovered she had disappeared to Miami. Before he could go down there for her, all hell broke loose.

Her replacement hero had turned out to be a villain.

His tongue found hers as he thrust inside her warm heat and they both moaned at the same time. An animalistic hunger took over, and he tightened his grip on her ass as he thrust into her harder, deeper, claiming her in a way he should have done lifetimes ago. With every stroke, every kiss, every caress, he dug deeper into her, until he was sure he'd disappear altogether and cease to exist.

And that was fine with him. He was man enough to admit he needed Chelsea by his side. She made him whole, and that had never been clearer than it was right now.

He moved his hips faster, harder, not even pausing when she came again, her tight walls closing around him. The faster he moved, the more she clung to him. As her nails scraped down his back, leaving scratches in their wake, she cried out as she orgasmed again, and this time, he was right there with her, soaring into the sky before gently drifting down, like snow. Dropping his forehead to hers, he breathed in deep, her scent filling his senses. "Chelsea…"

"You're wrong," she whispered, her hands tightening on his shoulders. "I do trust you."

He closed his eyes, drawing in a deep breath. "Then tell me—"

"Shh," she whispered, shaking her head. "Not now. Don't ruin it."

He felt way too damned good to care that, technically, she was still keeping her walls up. This was Chelsea, and she was the love of his life, and no matter what happened, he wasn't letting go of her again.

Not even when all his lies were revealed.

Chapter 21

I FINISHED DRYING my fake blond hair, staring at myself in the fogged-up mirror. My cheeks were flushed, and I swore I could still feel Jeremy touching me, making my body come alive with his soft, tender embrace. Everything about today had been perfect, which made me want to grin and uncharacteristically dance around in circles, but there was one thing holding me back from being happy.

Our relationship had an expiration date.

I wanted to selfishly spend as much time as possible with Jeremy, before it was all ripped away, but the game I played was a dangerous one. There were only two ways out, and one of them was a body bag.

I wasn't the type of person to focus on regrets, but right now? I had them. I had *lots* of them. If there was a way to go back, to not run away from the things I'd had all those years ago, I'd travel back in time in a split second. I'd stay by Jeremy's side and fight for him. I never would have gone to

Florida, or met Richard, or almost lost myself in his abuse. And I never would have had to kill him.

But regrets were as useless as dreams. I stared at myself in the mirror. For the first time in years, I liked what I saw, blond hair aside. I'd done a lot of bad things over the course of my life, but this time, I wasn't just moving forward. I was taking a stand to fix things. I was accepting responsibility for my actions, and I was righting the wrongs I'd inadvertently committed.

For the first time, I wasn't running from anything.

Not even Jeremy fricking Holland.

He knocked on the bathroom door. "You still showering, Chels?"

I lowered my fingers from my lips, eyeing my damp hair and the tiny towel wrapped around my body. My pulse sped up at the sound of his voice. "No, I'm out. You can come in."

Jeremy opened the door slowly, peeking his head through. When he saw me standing there in next to nothing, he tossed the envelope he'd been holding onto the counter, crossing the room with heated green eyes full of seduction. He wore a pair of sweats and nothing else.

He gripped the towel and raised a brow questioningly. I shrugged, and he undid the little knot I'd made to keep it in place. As the towel fell to the tile floor, he pulled me close, his hands resting on my ass, and whistled through his teeth.

I met his eyes in the mirror. A strand of hair fell over

his forehead, giving him a rakish appearance. He looked so happy, standing there holding me, that it physically hurt my heart. Looking away from our image, I buried my face in his bare chest and breathed him in like air, digging my fingers into the hard muscles of his back.

He gently tipped my face up to his, staring down at me for a second before he lowered his face to mine and kissed me tenderly. It took my breath away, that kiss. After his lips left mine, he released me, bending to pick up the towel he'd taken off me. "I didn't come in here to strip you, believe it or not."

I wrapped the towel around myself, trembling. "I wasn't exactly complaining," I said dryly.

"I know." He dragged his hand through his hair and reached for the envelope he'd tossed as he came in the room. "This came for you from the DMV."

My heart pounded in my ears, and I took it, feeling the envelope. Sure enough, something hard and rectangular was inside. "Oh."

He locked eyes with me, brushing my wet hair out of my face. "What's in it?"

"Nothing. It's nothing at all."

He frowned. "You're going to talk to me eventually."

"I know. Later." I bit my lip, staring up at him, making sure to hide any emotion. "Okay?"

For a second he looked disappointed, but then he gave me a tight smile and nodded. "All right. I'm going to hop in the shower. Want to go to Ollie's for dinner? We can get some takeout for Paul and swing by the hospital afterward. Then we need to go to Lowe's and pick out a chandelier for the foyer. Were you still thinking the elegant one, with the crystals and silver?"

"Yeah, I think that's the way to go. It'll match the old charm of the house."

He nodded. "And Chels—"

"I know," I said. "Later."

After the shower started, I took a second to grieve for what might have been, and then I tossed the envelope that held my new ID in the garbage, not even bothering to open it. There went my new start, in my inn and hometown, where I'd been planning to live with a real man by my side. I didn't need it anymore.

Because I wasn't getting it.

Chapter 22

WE GOT HOME really late, long after the moon had come out, when the sky had filled with stars. We'd been the last ones to check out at Lowe's after selecting the perfect chandelier that highlighted the comforts of modern style with an old-fashioned flair....

Which was exactly the effect that the inn would eventually have.

I stared up at the wires hanging from the ceiling and pictured the inn, in all its glory, once it was renovated, shiny, and open for business. Fixing up this place had given me a new purpose in life. It was exciting to build something real here in Hudson with my own two hands. I only wished I could finish what I'd started, but at least I had a man I could trust to see my vision through...even if I never got to see it for myself.

And that was fine. Or so I kept telling myself.

I'd run into Tommy McGinnis at Lowe's. I'd gone to school with him, and he'd been pretty thick with Paul.

They'd constantly caused trouble, like a pair of thieves… which they were. Last I heard, his wife left him and he was drowning his sorrows in heroin. Word was he was pretty much a lost cause…and that he was trying to drag my brother down with him. All the more reason I was happy Paul had insisted on going into protective custody with me. At least he wouldn't end up like Tommy. He'd be clean. Or as clean as two O'Kanes could get, anyway.

He'd promised when he asked to come along with me.

Jeremy set the chandelier down with a soft *oof*. "That shit's"—he kicked the door shut behind him and locked it—"a hell of a lot heavier than it looks."

"It's perfect."

"I agree." He craned his neck, glancing into the living room. "We totally could have gotten that second one tonight. It'll fit over the coffee table, for sure."

"Pick it up tomorrow for me, after work? Along with the carpet I was eyeing for the foyer."

"Of course." He stopped staring at the living room and focused those bright green eyes on me. He set his phone down on top of the box, his gaze locked on me. "We need to talk."

"Yeah. Okay."

"Don't look so scared. No matter what you tell me tonight, I'm not going anywhere." He smoothed my hair off my cheek. "I'm gonna grab a beer. Want one?"

I let out a soft breath, because *he* wasn't the one going somewhere. "Whiskey. Straight whiskey."

"Damn. That bad?"

I didn't say anything. Just stared at him. That was answer enough.

I knelt beside the chandelier box, looking at the picture on the side. Maybe we could get it hung up tonight before bed, so I could see it before I left. It was weird, but a melancholy acceptance had taken over, and I was almost...*numb*.

"So why are you racing the clock?" Jeremy called out from the kitchen.

I eyed the peach walls and the painted fireplace. "I started the paperwork to give you authorization over the inn and its accounts. Did your boss give the go-ahead for—?"

Jeremy's phone lit up on the box. Out of habit, I glanced down. It was a text message from someone named Vasquez. Need to update you on the Hudson project, call me immediately.

Vasquez...

Richard had employed a man with that last name, and he'd been even more ruthless than Richard. At first, I couldn't put two and two together as to why Vasquez would be texting Jeremy about a project, but some small part of me whispered, *Ha! I knew it all along! He was playing you.* And I couldn't shut that voice up once it came to life.

"For what?" he called out. "For me to take the inn on as a client?"

My heart pounded so hard it hurt. I stared at his phone, my finger itching to open it up and read more of those texts. Why was he getting messages from Vasquez? And why was he so insistent he stay here, by my side, the second I walked back into town? Jeremy didn't fit the profile of a cartel informant…which didn't make me feel better. If anything, it made me feel worse. Because I knew of a few occupations that used last names as much as they did first. Athletes, military…and *cops*. A perfectly respectable profession.

And that made a hell of a lot more sense than Jeremy being dirty.

The answer was blindingly obvious, and yet I didn't want to acknowledge it, because if he'd been lying to me this whole time—if he was a damn *cop*—then every ounce of trust I'd placed in his hands was complete and utter crap. I thought of the way he'd handled the gun the night we'd been shot at. His grip had been so sure, so comfortable, like he was around guns all the time. Like it was his *job*.

When I didn't answer, he came out into the foyer, scanning the room until he found me, sitting next to a box, looking lost as hell. The second we locked eyes, he froze, the smile slowly dying on his charming face. "Chels?"

Ah, the clever use of my childhood nickname, perfectly brought back into play so he could worm his way into my good graces. And the way he looked at me, like I mattered to him. Had he planned that, too? Was it the best way to make me, the gullible girl who was in love with him, jump back into his arms? I'd fallen for it, like the naïve little idiot I'd always been with him. Apparently years of distance hadn't changed that. All he had to do was kiss me, pretend he wanted me, and I became clay in his hands, waiting to be sculpted the way he wanted.

That son of a bitch.

"Who's Vasquez?" I asked, watching him closely for any signs of guilt.

He shifted on his feet, opened his mouth, closed it, and then pressed his lips together, his cheeks flushing ever so slightly as he turned away, hiding his face from me as he tried to come up with an answer I might believe.

Well. There you had it.

The guilt I'd been hoping not to see. It was written all over his damn face.

"Get out," I said, struggling to my feet, pulse racing, heart aching. "Get the hell out of my house *right now*."

Chapter 23

JEREMY STOOD THERE, staring at me, looking confused. What was there to be confused about? I told him to go, so he needed to leave. "What's wrong?" he finally asked.

"You tell me." I crossed my arms, gripping my elbows hard so I wouldn't launch myself at him and take him down. "Or better yet, don't. Just go. Tell your boss you failed to con me. I saw through your lies and kicked you out, *cop*."

He set the drinks down and walked toward me, making me stiffen. I didn't want him close to me. If he touched me... "Chels—"

"Oh, and FYI?" I picked up his phone and hurled it at him. He caught it easily, making me want to punch him even more. It would have been so much more satisfying if he hadn't. "There's an option on iPhones to make the text in a message not appear on the lock screen. Since you're trying to trick women into spilling information while undercover, you might want to use it."

He pinched the bridge of his nose. "I can explain."

"Yeah, I'm sure you can," I said sarcastically. "And I'm sure you're also convinced you can put a spin on this so I'll magically forgive you, and I don't blame you for thinking that, considering our history. Something like, 'I was trying to save you. To help you.'"

His jaw flexed. "It's the truth."

"Yeah. Sure it is."

He reached for my arm, but I lurched back. "Damn it, Chels. You know me. I didn't come here to hurt you. I've been watching—"

"You're a *cop*." I shook my head, backing away from him, my eyes burning. "What the hell, Jeremy? Why didn't you tell me?"

"Actually, I'm not a cop," he said, dragging his hand through his hair. "I'm DEA."

I threw my hands up. "Doesn't matter who signs your checks, you're law enforcement."

"Look, I *am* here to help you." He caught my hand, not letting go when I tried to tug free. His skin on mine, after finding out he'd been using me, felt wrong. "I'm not the enemy. I lo—"

"Tell me, were you laughing at how easy it was for me to believe you came back to me, after all these years, begging to be mine? Did you and all your little agent friends laugh at me when I kissed you in your motel room? Did you strategize together about how to pump me for information? Did they give you shit when you freaking *begged* me to let you in, to trust you? I bet that was a laugh. And when you got me to have sex with you again? Well, that must've been a real bonus."

His cheeks flushed. "Damn it, Chels. You know I wouldn't do that to you, or use you like that."

"Do I?"

"Damn right you do. I was protecting you even though you refused to tell me what happened between you and Richard. Even though you lied to me, time and time again, I stood here, watching your back—"

I laughed. Legit laughed. "You're going to try to lecture me about lying? Seriously?"

"Yes." He grabbed my shoulders gently, his touch burning right through my T-shirt. "And when your brother was attacked, I made sure he had a guard, that he had protection, even though you wouldn't tell me a damn thing about what happened or what you know. Why else would a mugging warrant police protection?"

"Well, that was all for nothing," I said, jerking free. "Why bother pushing me to open up, to reveal all my secrets in the first place? You already know what I did, don't you?"

He remained silent, not bothering to lie again. That was all the answer I needed.

"That's what I thought. You know the truth. I killed a man. I shot him where he stood, and I watched the blood soak the carpet as his body went limp." I pointed to the door, trembling slightly. "Get out before I kill you, too."

Chapter 24

HE REARED BACK, staring at me like I'd punched him in the gut. Which I guess I had, in a way. I'd threatened to kill him—not that I actually would. "Chels—"

"You have no idea how angry I am right now. I killed Richard, is that what you want to hear? I pulled the trigger, and he stopped breathing in front of me. And you know what? I'm not sorry. Things were great at first, but he became an abusive bastard. When I found out he was working with a cartel, compromising cases so their guys would walk, that was the last straw. I was going to leave him quietly, but he came at me and I grabbed the gun, and I—" I broke off, choking back a sob, hating myself for that sign of weakness but unable to take it back. "So you see, bad things happen to people who lie to me."

He swallowed hard, stepping closer despite my threats. "Chelsea, please, let me—"

"You know what the worst part was? I was going to tell you tonight. Tell you everything. I wanted to be honest because I…" The fire of rage inside me transformed into the cold of heartbreak. I wasn't sure I'd ever be warm again. "I was going to be honest. And you've been lying to me, playing me, all this time."

He shook his head, taking another step toward me. "Chels, you have to understand, the DEA had you flagged as a person of interest. Richard had been under investigation and they weren't sure how complicit you were. After the shooting, I got involved to *protect* you. I convinced my superiors that our preexisting relationship made me the perfect person to send in, but it was always my intention to get you clear of this."

"Right." I laughed, but it wasn't a laugh. Not really. I'd obviously been nothing but a damsel in distress to him. Wasn't he surprised to find himself defending the dragon? "And the part about missing me? Wanting me to be with you?"

"True," he said quickly. "I did miss you. A lot."

"Yeah. Sure." I rubbed my face. My eyes burned and my throat ached, unfamiliar sensations for me. "You're a DEA agent, Jeremy. I was a 'person of interest.' You knew where I was. You could've ridden your white horse down to Miami at any time."

"I did look for you, but you'd covered your tracks too well. By the time I found you…" He shook his head, reaching for me again. I shifted back, not letting him touch me. Those days were over. *"Chelsea."*

"Let me guess. You're up for some sort of promotion, once this is over?" I asked slowly. "If you arrest me or I help you get the bad guy?"

He rubbed the back of his neck, shifting uncomfortably. That gave me my answer.

"You really think I'm doing this because it'll benefit me? No, I'm doing it for the seventeen-year-old Long Island girl who overdosed on heroin. For the mother of two in Philadelphia who died when her car was T-boned by a driver high on cocaine. For the family who got caught in the crossfire of a drug war in Boston." His shoulders were hard, and his entire body was tense. I couldn't help but wonder if *I* was his enemy now. "We've been investigating these guys for years, working with local PDs as they scoop up the small fish, but we're after the head. The leader of the cartel has a brother who's a total mess. The only thing he's good at is taking care of people who become problems. When you took out Richard, you became a problem."

"You're hoping that he's such a disaster that he'll turn on his brother. So, what, you leaked my general whereabouts and used me as bait for this asshole, never thinking I might just want to keep my head down and live my life? You put my brother in danger? When exactly were you going to arrest the guy? Before or after he tortured me, too?" I rubbed my throbbing temples.

Jeremy reacted like I'd stabbed him, his body jerking slightly. His hand reached out to me. "I told you, I came here to protect you. I would never let *anyone* hurt you."

I pointedly ignored his hand, and he let it drop to the back of a floral upholstered loveseat. "Should I presume that my arrest would soon follow Javi's? Or is the warrant already waiting, just in case I discovered the truth?"

He pressed his lips together. "I've been authorized to offer you a deal—"

"What was the plan for the inn?" I asked, cutting him off, my voice hard. Frozen solid. "Was it going to be seized? Or would you let me make you a signatory, keep it as part of your cover, and use it as some secret DEA safe house?"

Jeremy went to answer and then paused for a moment. "Wait a second. How did you know Javi's name?"

Oh, look, the DEA agent was back.

I turned away, staring at the divots in the wall where Jeremy had plastered the bullet holes. "I'm the daughter of a con man, Jeremy. Dad always said to have either an exit strategy or a will. I couldn't just break up with Richard; his pride would never allow that. I was preparing to blackmail him in exchange for my freedom. It was easy to gather the proof I needed, once I knew where to look for it, because he never saw me as a viable threat. Sometimes he even took meetings at the house. So, yes, I know Javi, and Gabriel, and David. I know them all. But more importantly, I know where the money goes."

Jeremy moved around that loveseat fast. He stood in front of me, catching himself before he grabbed my shoulders. "Chels, this is huge. With this proof, we could arrest them all now. You and Paul would be safe."

I shifted my head slightly so I could continue staring at the wall. "Funnily enough, I wasn't that concerned with my own safety when I made the deal with Homeland Security. I'll turn over the evidence for immunity and Witness Protection. *I* was trying to protect *you*."

He instinctively reached for his pocket, as if to go for his phone. "You made a deal with Homeland? I wasn't informed."

"So much for interagency cooperation." I walked over to the front door and finally met his gaze. "Get out."

The last time I saw that expression on his face, it was after Rocco, his dog, passed away. I refused to be moved. "We can figure something out. Witness Protection doesn't have to be the end of us."

"It wasn't. We ended when you decided to play me instead of telling me the truth and asking for my help. I tried really hard to live in your world, Jeremy, to do what's right, but in the end, all you saw was a criminal," I said, my voice cracking on the last word. More weakness. And it was all Jeremy fricking Holland's fault. "I thought you were one of the good guys. Thanks for proving to me that good guys don't just finish last—they don't exist at all."

I knew my words hit home for Jeremy because he rubbed his chest right over his heart. "I'm sorry. I never wanted to hurt you."

"Yeah. That's what they all say." Opening the door, I met his eyes again, forcing my chin up. "Get. Out."

Jeremy headed for the door, looking like a lost puppy being sent back out into the rain. He stopped just outside. "This isn't over. I'm going to go find out the particulars of your deal. I'll be back tomorrow. I let you run from me once, but that's not happening again."

There it was again. That stubborn determination to win me back. It wouldn't work this time. He'd done me dirty, and I wouldn't forget it. "I'm not running anywhere, Agent Holland. Like the O'Kane family motto, I'm gonna keep moving forward. Without you." And then I slammed the door in his face. "Asshole."

I waited till I heard his car start, till the headlights receded down the driveway, and till I felt his absence down to my soul. Then, and only then, I let myself slide down the door into a sitting position. My eyes burned but they were dry. The *one* man I thought who wouldn't break me, who wouldn't *use* me, had done exactly that.

Go figure.

I stared out into the living room, at the half-finished promise of what the inn could be. A respite from stress, an oasis of calm, a sanctuary, never fulfilled. I should have known better. Every time I tried to do something good, it went to shit. I was done fighting, done trying to be better. Being something I wasn't.

I was *me*.

And nothing would ever change that.

Chapter 25

I WENT TO the hospital and told Paul everything, explaining Jeremy's deception. He was not pleased in the least, but he promised to make sure that, before we left town, the inn would be taken care of for me through some legit contacts of his. And unlike *some* people in my life, when my brother made a promise, he kept it. He also promised to have his people make Jeremy's life a living hell, but I told him not to bother. Jeremy had just been doing his job. If he'd really cared about me like he'd claimed, he would've approached the situation differently.

Maybe he'd just never known me at all.

Either way, he didn't deserve my brother breathing down his neck. Witness Protection might make Paul legit, but he would still have friends in low places.

Then I went back to the inn to say good-bye for the last time. The work on the living room was almost finished. The furniture I'd picked out would be delivered Monday, and Paul had promised to have his guy place it according to the floor plan I'd drawn on a napkin, using the fireplace as a focal point. The antique white fireplace stood out against the pale walls, and the hardwood floors shined with the fresh coats of varnish we'd put on after Jeremy had sanded them. The sun shone in the windows, reflecting off the shiny floor, and the room was as bright and inviting as I'd imagined it would be.

I swallowed hard at the ache in my chest that had never fully gone away since the other night. I headed for the kitchen, taking in the detailing on the moldings. Now that the DEA knew everything, things had started to move along quickly. However, the closer I got to the kitchen, the more cautious I grew. The air smelled like spaghetti sauce, and soft classical music played from my bedroom. I hadn't made any sauce, or left the radio on….

"Jeremy?" I called out, my heart racing.

Knowing he was here, waiting for me to come home as if nothing had happened, made me equal parts nervous and angry. When I found him, I was gonna kick his ass. I knew that with one look at him, the chemistry between us would roar back to life, but I'd be strong and resist him this time.

No one answered as I entered the kitchen, staring at the sauce. It bubbled slowly, painting the glass lid with little spurts of red. There was a bouquet of red roses on the counter, and the combination of the red sauce and the red roses set me on edge. Jeremy knew I didn't like roses any longer, and, despite his terrible lies, he'd never remind me of the abusive dead ex-boyfriend I'd killed.

I made my way to the front door, walking slowly, heart pounding with fear. Even though it might seem crazy to think that Javi had broken into my home to make spaghetti sauce and turn on Mozart...I knew, I just *knew,* that something was wrong. I'd never doubted my instincts before, and since they'd saved my life more than once, I wasn't about to start now.

I opened the drawer with my gun inside it slowly, lifting the Glock cautiously as I made my way up the stairs. I could leave, call Jeremy for help, but I was done leaning on other people for support. I'd taken care of Richard all on my own—I could handle Javi, too. Each step I took brought me closer to whatever waited for me up there. Whether it was Javi or Jeremy, there was going to be a fight.

The second-to-last step creaked as I put my weight on it, and I froze. The gun wavered, and I tightened my grip on it, trying to talk myself down. I was probably overreacting. Maybe it was Jeremy in my bedroom, putting together some grand romantic gesture, like sprinkling flower petals on my bed. Maybe this would all be a bad daydream.

There was no way in hell I'd call out his name again...just in case. I crept around the corner of the hallway, keeping an eye out for movement from any other rooms along the way. I passed Jeremy's, which was empty, and sucked in a deep breath at the entrance to my room.

The door was cracked open, and I saw a brown-haired male, his head lowered as he sat on my bed. The very sight sent a chill down my spine.

Because that hair…I knew it.

I'd run my fingers through it, once upon a time.

Biting down on my lip, I stepped forward, my knuckles aching and my heart pounding. My weapon wobbled in concert with my trembling body, as I nudged the door open with my foot. It creaked and the man lifted his head, locking eyes with me.

My gaze met brown eyes. Dark, soulless ones. His jaw was hard and unbreakable.

"No," I whispered, staring with horror at the man on my bed as my stomach turned. "You're…you're…"

"Dead? Sorry to disappoint." Richard gave me a small smile. One I recognized all too well. He usually smiled like that before he "corrected me."

No. No, no, no, *hell, no*. He was supposed to be *dead*. I'd killed him. Watched him hit the floor, not moving, as blood sprayed from his chest. *This couldn't be…*

Shaking my head, I aimed the gun at his chest and did the only thing I could do, given the situation. The only thing I could think of that might save my ass.

I pulled the trigger again.

Chapter 26

THE RESOUNDING CLICK of the striker was the only sound that filled the room, somehow managing to seem louder than an actual gunshot. I choked on a half laugh, half sob, because *of course* Richard had taken care of my only weapon. He wasn't about to be taken down by the same weapon, or person, twice.

He tugged on his tie to straighten it. "I wasn't sure if you had the balls to pull that trigger again, but you understand my hesitation to find out firsthand."

"Go to hell. I should have known the devil couldn't be taken down by a bullet."

He laughed, pressing a hand to his flat stomach. He looked so handsome standing there, laughing as if everything were normal. That had always been one of his best weapons. His good looks. He used them well. "I don't know whether to be insulted or flattered."

"I don't care how you feel anymore."

"Tell me, have you been having fun, playing house with

that man? What's his name? Ah, yes, Agent Jeremy Holland." When I stiffened, he locked eyes with me.

Shit. He knew Jeremy's name.

"Don't tell me you think I haven't been watching you with him. Kissing him. Fucking him. Letting him take what's mine."

I stepped forward, muscles tight, fists even tighter. The second I took a step toward him, someone grabbed me from behind by both arms. Of course. Richard was too much of a coward to take me on alone. "I'm not yours. I stopped being yours the second I realized you were nothing but a scared little boy, kowtowing to the cartel so they didn't kill you. Tell me, did you agree to be their bitch before or after you took office? I'm dying to know."

"You little—" He lifted his hand threateningly, the backs of the knuckles facing me, and I flinched reflexively. Being backhanded hurt more than being punched with a closed fist, and he knew it. "You have no idea what you're talking about. *I'm* the one with the power. *I'm* the one who controls them, not the other way around. Why do you think they're here with me, hunting down you and everyone you ever loved?"

I didn't flinch. Just stared him in the eye. "Luckily for you, you never fell in that category."

He snorted. "You loved me. Did you get my flowers? I left the last ones on your bed as a reminder of who you belong to."

Knowing he'd been in my room made my stomach turn hard. "Yeah. I got them. And I threw them in the trash," I said from between clenched teeth.

Running his hand over his jaw, he eyed me, grinning like the calm maniac he was. "I admire your spunk. It's a shame you had to try to kill me. You would have made an excellent wife. But now I have to kill you because if you're not an asset, then you're a liability."

"What makes you think my death will change anything? That I haven't already given the feds everything?"

"I have my ways." He shrugged casually as he rolled up his shirtsleeves. He did it calmly and without emotion, even though we both knew what was coming. I'd found out firsthand how much he liked playing with his toys before breaking them. "And your lover won't be an issue."

Cold fear struck my heart, sending a shaft of pain piercing through my chest. I knew better than to fall for that shit, but at the same time...this was Jeremy we were talking about. God, if he hurt him, it would be all my fault, and a world without Jeremy wasn't a world I wanted to be in. He might have lied to me and I might be pissed as hell at him, but I loved him with all my heart. And I wanted the chance to maybe forgive him someday, after a hell of a lot of groveling on his part.

I needed him to be okay.

"You're lying," I said with a confidence I didn't feel.

He shrugged again, finishing up with his sleeve. The second it was perfectly in place above his elbows, he took a step in my direction. I jerked hard, trying to break free of my captor, knowing it was pointless to do so. I caught sight of Javi's profile over my shoulder and it was clear there'd be no escape.

"Jeremy will figure out where I hid everything. It's in the hiding place from when we were kids," I said in a rush, lying through my teeth in a futile attempt to buy time. "You're too late."

"We both know that's not true. Let's not diminish your spirit with useless lies and pleas for mercy. You're a fighter, Chelsea. We both enjoy that."

I glared at him silently, heart pounding against my ribs.

"This is going to hurt me more than it hurts you, darling," Richard said softly, his voice like warm butter spreading on fresh-baked bread. "But I need to teach you a lesson. By the time I'm done, you'll wish you never let another man touch what belonged to me. And maybe, if you're lucky, I won't kill you. Maybe I'll take you back, if you promise to never cheat on me again."

The crazy thing was, he meant every word. Richard honestly thought I'd want to be with him, completely ignoring the fact I'd tried to kill him. How had my life gotten to this? How did I become prey to this bastard?

The abuse had started slowly. It had been emotional at first, delivered so craftily I didn't even notice it until it was too late. When that stopped working, he became violent.

A push here, followed by an apology. A slap there, followed up with flowers and words of love.

That's when I'd started planning my escape. I'd rediscovered my strength when I came here, to this inn. When I'd pulled that trigger and put an end to the abuse.

I'd be *damned* if I lost that strength again.

"I doubt I'll go back to you," I said sweetly. "After all, you're nothing but a spineless, wormy coward who has no idea what it's like to be a real man. Jeremy knows how to treat a woman, and he knows how to be a man, so I'd never regret being with him. Only you. I wish I never let you touch me, and I wish you had died when I shot you."

Finally, for the first time ever, he lost his cool. Anger flushed his cheeks, his upper lip curled, and he growled. Hauling his fist back, he let it fly, and pain burst in my skull, making me crumble in Javi's arms. Stars exploded into my vision.

"Drop her," Richard said.

Javi obeyed immediately, and I hit the floor hard, banging my head. Suddenly, Richard was on top of me. "Take it back."

Unable to speak, I did the one thing I knew would piss him off, because, God, I wanted to get under his skin…I laughed, spitting out blood with the sound.

Right in his face.

An animalistic sound escaped him, and his eyes bulged in rage as he stared down at me, unable to believe I'd disobeyed him. He lifted his hand and slapped me with his knuckles. I weakly pushed at his shoulders, but Javi pinned down my arms before I could get any leverage. I let out a loud scream, my one last attempt at freedom, but then his hand was on my throat, cutting off my air supply, and I knew with a sinking clarity that this was it.

And then the blackness took over.

Chapter 27

JEREMY WAS STEPS from the front door of the inn when he heard it. A fall leaf crunched behind him, and a soft breath was released. The hair on the back of his neck rose, and every instinct he'd ever trusted told him danger approached. He dropped the chandelier to the ground with a crash and spun with his gun drawn.

The man creeping up behind him froze for a split second, which is the only reason Jeremy didn't end up with a bullet in his brain. Unlike the other man, he didn't hesitate—his finger squeezed the trigger and the guy went down with a hit to his chest. Jeremy stared at him. It didn't take a genius to figure out the man was in the cartels.

"Shit," he muttered. "Fueller? You out there?"

There was no answer from the agent on duty. Jeremy scanned the trees as he picked up the dead man's gun and tucked it in the waistband of his jeans. Finally he saw Fueller. He was on his back in the shadows, blood congealing on the ground from a bullet wound to the head.

Cursing, Jeremy made a phone call to request backup and then wasted no time approaching the inn on light feet. Knowing Chelsea might be inside made him want to run up the stairs screaming her name, but that wouldn't do either of them any good.

His pulse pounded. He should have come earlier, damn it, but he'd been trying to give her some time to cool off. She had every right to be angry, but he knew he had to get past that anger and find a way to make her see he hadn't been lying to her about everything. He did love her, and he had no intention of giving up on her…again.

After a few more steps, he was in the foyer. The door was ajar, and he scanned the interior for any signs of intrusion. The table drawer by the door was open, and Chelsea's gun was gone. The second he stepped into the living room, he saw another cartel foot soldier. He stood guard over the kitchen, watching the back door.

Well, that was a good sign.

It meant he was counting on the dead guy out front to stop anyone from coming in, and he was watching the back. Hopefully, there would be no one else to contend with. Tucking his gun away, Jeremy crept up and locked his arm around the man's throat, taking him down effectively and silently. The asshole struggled for a good five seconds, arms flailing, but it was a useless fight. Jeremy wasn't letting go till he was unconscious or dead.

Either one worked for him.

The second he went limp, Jeremy lowered him to the floor. At the same time, Chelsea let out a scream. He bolted up the stairs, not bothering to be quiet anymore, not even debating whether or not to wait for his backup, skidding into her bedroom with his gun aimed for anything that wasn't *her*. He'd seen a lot of messed-up shit during his time as a DEA agent, but the sight that met his eyes was horrifying.

Something he would *never* forget.

Chelsea was on the floor, and someone was on top of her, choking her. She struggled against her assailant, but her movements were slowing. Another knelt at her head, holding her shoulders down as the other man attacked her viciously. The amount of rage that slammed into Jeremy was unreal, and he saw red.

Literally. Blood *red*.

He recognized Javi as the man holding her down. Javi glanced up, spotting him, and cursed. Releasing Chelsea's shoulders, he pulled out a gun and took aim. Jeremy did the same. He didn't hesitate or think like an agent in that moment. He just pulled the goddamn trigger and took the asshole down.

Javi was hit between the eyes, but not before he could squeeze off a shot. Jeremy staggered back, pain ripping through his body, but he didn't take a second to recover. He didn't have time. He turned to Chelsea, who was struggling under her attacker with renewed fervor, and when he glanced at him…

Richard wasn't dead.

This changed everything. If they managed to take him down without killing him, Chelsea would be a free woman. Richard would probably do anything to save his own skin and they could use his testimony to replace whatever evidence Chelsea had. This whole thing could be over.

Chelsea punched Richard in the face with an impressive upper-cut, and the asshole reared back, blood spurting out of his nose. She squirmed out of his arms, struggling to reach the gun lying on the floor. Richard grabbed his nose, cursing. "I'll kill you, you little bitch."

"DEA, asshole. Don't move," Jeremy said, aiming at Richard, who'd been was so focused on hurting Chelsea that he'd ignored the gunplay three feet away. "One move and you're a dead man."

Richard froze, watching him carefully, his gaze finally leaving Chelsea. He seethed with a cold, calculated rage. "You're a federal agent. I'm unarmed. You can't just shoot me."

"Try me." His finger flexed on the trigger. "Chels, are you okay?"

"Yes," she croaked. She cocked the gun in her hand and Jeremy stiffened. "But *he* won't be."

Jeremy tore his eyes off the man and stared at Chelsea.

"Go ahead," Richard taunted, holding his arms to his sides. "Shoot an unarmed man. That one's actually loaded."

She stood up on unsteady feet, swaying, and pointed the gun at Richard. Blood trickled out her nose and from the corner of her split lip, and bruises were already forming around her neck. Her eyes held a light that warned that she was close to the edge and not thinking clearly. He'd seen that look in plenty of people's eyes before. She was going to take any chance at freedom she had, and nothing he said was going to stop her.

Downstairs, men came into the house, calling out to one another that it was clear. His backup was here, just in time to witness this. If Chelsea killed Richard now, no amount of maneuvering on Jeremy's part would save her.

Chapter 28

RICHARD WAS JUST staring at me with that goddamn cocky smirk, kneeling on the floor with my blood smeared on his knuckles, so sure I wouldn't do it. That I wouldn't put an end to his pathetic excuse of a life. Right now, there was nothing I wanted more in this life than to end his. Murder hadn't been part of my original plan, but Dad always said that you had to be ready to improvise.

If I didn't kill him now, what would stop him from coming back in a year, or five, or ten, to finish what he'd started? No. Never again.

I tightened my finger on the trigger.

"No!" Jeremy shouted out, holding a hand in front of him as he approached slowly. "DEA is here, right downstairs. If you pull that trigger, you'll go to jail, Chels. Your immunity agreement won't save you. Your hands are clean right now. You didn't kill him before, and you don't have to kill him now."

I didn't ease up, and my eyes burned with the force of

the tears I held back. Angry tears that screamed to be released. Tears I'd been holding back for longer than I could remember. "I don't care. He'll be dead. That's all that matters."

"That's not all that matters. There's the inn. And there's..." He tucked his gun away, waving off the men standing behind me. Clearly they were standing there ready to take Richard away—or take me down. "There's me. I love you, Chels."

I swallowed hard. "Don't lie to me again, Agent Holland."

"I'm not," he said slowly. "I'm telling the truth. Yes, I lied to you about my occupation. Yes, you have every right to be angry at me and to hate me, but damn it, Chels, give me a chance to earn your forgiveness. I'll never stop trying, and I'll never stop knocking on your door, asking you to let me in. But if you're in jail...we don't stand a chance in hell in making this thing we have between us work.

"He wants you to kill him because it keeps him from retribution from the cartel, and it ruins your life. It's a win-win for him," Jeremy said in a rush. He stepped closer, putting himself between me and Richard but not moving to take the gun from me. Blood soaked his shirt at the shoulder. I stared at the spot, watching the red spread across his blue shirt. "Don't give him that satisfaction. Don't give him what he wants."

My grip on the gun wavered, and I sensed men creeping

closer behind me, waiting to take me down if I didn't give up the gun soon. I had a feeling the only reason they hadn't yet was because of Jeremy. "But he'll come back if I don't kill him. Just like he did this time."

"No, he won't. He's going to jail."

I heard the words he said, but I didn't have much faith in the criminal justice system to keep him there. I'd seen too much to believe that it would all be okay.

"He's still alive, Chels. If you keep him that way, you're free." Jeremy held his hands up, locking eyes with me, looking a little ashen. "You can rebuild the inn. You can be here, like you wanted, with a new life. And I'll be here with you, helping. I swear to God, I will be here."

I bit my lip, swaying slightly. "Don't think you're off the hook. You lied to me. I'm still pissed at you."

"I know. I swear, I'll make it up to you. Every second of every day, I'll make it up to you." He shot a nervous look behind me. "Just put the gun down."

Chapter 29

I LOWERED MY arm slowly, releasing the trigger and exhaling at the same time, my throat aching because of Richard's abuse. "Take him away."

I didn't even look at Richard. Didn't give him the satisfaction. I just stared at Jeremy as the men who had hovered behind me rushed forward, taking Richard away in cuffs. Once we were alone, I wrapped my arms around myself, my whole body aching from the beating and the fight I'd lived through. But it was over now. It was actually over. "You're shot."

Jeremy glanced down. "Yeah. It's nothing."

I didn't say anything to that because it didn't look like *nothing* to me. "So now what?"

"Now—*Christ*." He crossed the room, closing the distance between us. He pulled me into his arms, threaded his hands in my hair, and kissed me gently. I was pissed at him, and there were a million reasons why I shouldn't be in his arms like this. But right now? I needed him more than I needed air. When he pulled back, he framed my face with his hands gently. "Now we get checked out by a doctor, and then we come home. I'll tuck you in and stay the night to make sure no one bothers you for at least twenty-four hours. You need to recover from today."

His voice was raspy at the end. Almost broken.

"You think you're staying the night?" I asked. "Hell no. I'm fine on my—"

"It wasn't a request. I'm staying." He ran his thumb over my cheek, smiling gently when I glowered at him. "I meant what I said before all this went down. I'm not going anywhere, Chels. I know this scares you, and you don't feel the same way yet, and I know you're pissed as hell at me, but I love you. I'm going to spend the rest of my life loving you, even if you never forgive me or love me back. And nothing you do or say will stop me."

I stared up at him, heart pounding. For the first time, hearing those words come out of his mouth and seeing him look at me like I was his whole world didn't make me want to run. It made me want to *stay*. We had a lot to resolve between us, but at the end of the day, it had always been…and would always be…Jeremy fricking Holland. I could have it all. The inn. The man. The life I'd always wanted.

And suddenly, it didn't seem too crazy to let myself feel that way.

"I love you, too," I said, my voice more of a whisper than anything.

His eyes widened. "What?"

"I love you," I said again, this time with more strength behind the words. "But I'm still mad at you for lying to me," I added for good measure.

He laughed, and he kissed me again, this time in a promise of forever, and of what was to come. And I believed every single second of it. I'd finally found my home.

It was with him, in Maine, all along.

About the Author

JEN McLAUGHLIN is a *New York Times* and *USA Today* bestselling romance author. She was mentioned in *Forbes* alongside E. L. James as one of the breakout independent authors to dominate the bestseller lists. She is represented by Louise Fury at the Bent Agency. She loves hearing from her fans, and you can visit her on the web at JenMcLaughlin.com.

LOOKING TO FALL IN LOVE IN JUST ONE NIGHT?

INTRODUCING BOOKSHOTS FLAMES:

original romances presented by James Patterson that fit into your busy life.

FEATURING LOVE STORIES BY:

New York Times bestselling author Jen McLaughlin

New York Times bestselling author Samantha Towle

USA Today bestselling author Erin Knightley

Elizabeth Hayley

Jessica Linden

Codi Gary

Laurie Horowitz

…and many others!

AVAILABLE FROM

"ALEX CROSS, I'M COMING FOR YOU...."

Gary Soneji, the killer from *Along Came a Spider,* has been dead for more than ten years—but Cross swears he saw Soneji gun down his partner. Is Cross's worst enemy back from the grave?

Nothing will prepare you for the wicked truth.

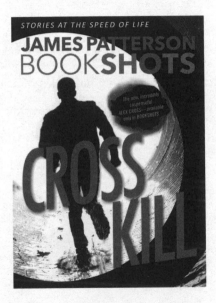

Read the next riveting, pulse-racing Alex Cross adventure, available only from

BOOKSHOTS

"I'M NOT ON TRIAL. SAN FRANCISCO IS."

Drug cartel boss the Kingfisher has a reputation for being violent and merciless. And after he's finally caught, he's set to stand trial for his vicious crimes—until he begins unleashing chaos and terror upon the lawyers, jurors, and police associated with the case. The city is paralyzed, and Detective Lindsay Boxer is caught in the eye of the storm.

Will the Women's Murder Club make it out alive—or will a sudden courtroom snare ensure their last breaths?

Read the shocking new Women's Murder Club story, available only from

BOOK**SHOTS**

WILL THE LAST HUMANS ON EARTH PLEASE TURN OUT THE LIGHTS?

As humans continue to be plagued by vicious animal attacks, zoologist Jackson Oz desperately tries to save the ones he loves—and the rest of mankind. But animals aren't the only threat anymore. Some *humans* are starting to evolve too, turning into something feral and ferocious....

Could this savage new species save civilization—or end it?

Read the high-adrenaline page-turner *Zoo II,* available only from

BOOK**SHOTS**

MICHAEL BENNETT FACES HIS TOUGHEST CASE YET....

Detective Michael Bennett is called to the scene after a man plunges to his death outside a trendy Manhattan hotel—but the man's fingerprints are traced to a pilot who was killed in Iraq years ago.

Will Bennett discover the truth?

Or will he become tangled in a web of government secrets?

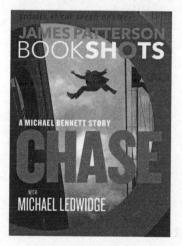

Read the new action-packed Michael Bennett story,
Chase, **coming soon from**

BOOK**SHOTS**

SOME GAMES AREN'T FOR CHILDREN....

After a nasty divorce, Christy Moore finds her escape in Marty Hawking, who introduces her to all sorts of new experiences, including an explosive new game called "Make-Believe."

But what begins as innocent fun soon turns dark, and as Marty pushes the boundaries further and further, the game may just end up deadly.

**Read the white-knuckle thriller,
coming soon from**

BOOK**SHOTS**

CAN A LITTLE BLACK DRESS CHANGE EVERYTHING?

Divorced magazine editor Jane Avery is content with spending her nights alone—until she finds *The Dress*. Suddenly she's surrendering to dark desires, and New York City has become her erotic playground. But what begins as a sultry fantasy has gone too far....

And her next conquest could be her last.

Check out the steamy cliffhanger *Little Black Dress*, coming soon from

BOOK**SHOTS**